CHAOS AND FLAMES

The Complete Series

Evelyn Winters

Copyright © 2020 Evelyn Winters

All rights reserved

The characters and events portrayed in this book are fictitious. Any similarity to real persons, living or dead, is coincidental and not intended by the author.

No part of this book may be reproduced, or stored in a retrieval system, or transmitted in any form or by any means, electronic, mechanical, photocopying, recording, or otherwise, without express written permission of the publisher.

Cover design by: Ammelor Rae

CONTENTS

Title Page	
Copyright	
The Dragon's Gift	1
Chapter One	3
Chapter Two	10
Chapter Three	25
Chapter Four	40
Chapter Five	53
Chapter Six	62
Chapter Seven	74
Chapter Eight	87
The Dragon's War	99
Chapter One	101
Chapter Two	113
Chapter Three	126
Chapter Four	138
Chapter Five	149

Chapter Six	162
Chapter Seven	173
Chapter Eight	183
The Dragon's Return	189
Chapter 1	191
Chapter 2	204
Chapter 3	217
Chapter 4	228
Chapter 5	236
Chapter 6	253
Chapter 7	263
Chapter 8	275
Bonus Short: James and Kieran's Story	285
About The Author	293
Books By This Author	295

THE DRAGON'S GIFT

Chaos and Flames Book 1

> I threw myself into that fire, threw myself into it, into him, and let myself burn.
> ~Sarah J. Maas, **A Court of Thorns and Roses**

CHAPTER ONE

Thunder boomed across the stormy night's sky, rattling the chandelier hanging in Alina's spacious drawing room. When she signed the lease on this state of the arc penthouse apartment, she never considered what it would be like to experience a thunderstorm from the top story of a skyscraper. The results were terrifyingly beautiful. The space around her was floor to ceiling windows, accentuating the dark, swirling purple of the clouds and every burst of lightening across the sky. She felt as if she had been shoved right into the eye of the storm itself. Another clap of thunder crashed across the sky and she was thankful for the thick, impervious windows around her apartment. She doubted they would ever rattle or shake like the ones in her previous apartment had. Of course, that apartment was a second story, run down college apartment that she'd kept ever since she started university. Even though it had been ten years since moving into that place, she still remembered how it felt to be leaving home and to have an apartment of her own for the first time.

Another crack of thunder shook her from her

memories. The day that was supposed to be one of the proudest moments of her life, along with graduating with her degree in business, was shadowed by the events that arose in that apartment. It wasn't the first time something on the supernatural side happened to her, but it was the only time she felt uneasy or worse, afraid for her life. She had felt eyes following her everywhere in that apartment and could never escape the feeling of being watched. Her friends just thought it was the paranoia getting to her, living alone for the first time, but her college friends didn't know she was used to being alone. She was orphaned at the age of three and couldn't even summon a picture of her parents from memory if she tried.

Coming back to reality, surrounded by an expensive penthouse with an open floor plan and expensive electronic gadgets tastefully hidden among the modern, dark décor, Alina was grateful that that time in her life was over. Her new place was spotless, another difference between her first apartment and her new home, and it was so big Alina briefly entertained the idea of hiring a cleaning lady. She might feel a little lazy about it but at least she could use her new fortune to give someone in need a job.

It was along the same lines of thinking that she used millions of her money to fund the new study program and interactive exhibit at Titan Labs. It was all being kept very "hush hush" until the official release to the public. Besides, what good was billions if you couldn't find out a few secrets in the human genome or maybe the cure for cancer. The liaison from the labs had promised her that the findings from this study could change the course of history.

The world's last dragon shifter. A creature many thought to be extinct, alongside the dinosaurs, but scientists found one hiding deep inside Northern Europe. She bid alongside several other billionaires for the chance to be the sole patron of the exhibit and despite being "new money," she won. When the lab director, a Mr. Simon Aldridge, said it would take several million to build an exhibit with the size and the strength they'd need to contain the creature, let alone the cost of the actual clinical studies on it, many of the others backed out. That was one thing Alina never understood about the wealthy: they were so afraid to part with their money.

Alina sighed, pacing across her open living room into her enormous kitchen, stopping next to her stainless-steel refrigerator. She opened and closed it a few times, taking in the neat little stacks of prepared meals in plastic containers, each labeled with a name and expiration date by her nutritionist/personal chef and wondered if she was becoming too dependent on her money. She shut her fridge again and refused to acknowledge the real reason she was acting so jumpy. She had a meeting with Simon Aldridge in the morning about the shifter exhibit and she was dreading what he was going to say. But why else would he call for a face to face meeting if he didn't have bad news to impart? Checking her phone and realizing it was only a quarter past eight, she resolved to distract herself. Marching into her bedroom, which was decorated much like the rest of her penthouse with modern features and dark colors, she texted her driver to pick her up in twenty minutes.

She studied herself in the floor to ceiling mirror, thumbs threading through the loops of her black skinny jeans. She traded her top for one with a little more cleavage and lace, after only a little deliberation in her enormous walk in closet, light spilling out from the space to her bedroom floor. She passed rows of gowns, dresses, perfectly pressed business wear, and stacks of her favorite comfy pajamas until she reached the shoes. Rows of gleaming shined shoes formed a horseshoe shape around the back of her closet. She hopped between rooms with shoes and accessories in hand before finally deciding on a pair of sexy black pumps and some glittering silver earrings that she thought would look beautiful shining out of her dark hair.

She caught her private elevator down to the lobby of her building and wished the doorman a goodnight as she slipped into her private car. She told her driver to take her to a club and relished at the thought of spending the night surrounded by living, breathing people, instead of laying alone in her too big apartment waiting to fall asleep and start a new day. When she made it to the entrance, she was let inside immediately despite the line, the bodyguard aware that she was usually a big spender. It didn't hurt that she had her push-up bra on either. Music pulsed in time with her heartbeat as she pushed her way onto the dance floor, several bodies making way to allow her room.

She immediately found herself pressed against multiple bodies, tangling her limbs with others. She danced like this was her first night out, swayed to nameless songs and lets lyrics slip off her tongue while she shouted along. She ended up in a sea of people, but not just another face in the crowd. Most of the men on the dance floor angled themselves towards her, tried to seek her out and press against her moving body. Hands glide down her sides, lingered on her ass and hips, or slid up to cup her breasts, but none of it caught her attention. They slid off her like water from a ducks back. She gulped their free drinks, let them touch a little, but moved to another group of willing bodies when things started to get too heated.

She allowed them to touch because they're good-looking, but it all felt so fake to her. She left to distract herself from the worry but ended up feeling numb instead. None of these men want anything more than one night with her, maybe more once they found out about the money but none of it would be real. She breathed in the smell of sweat and perfume, cologne, and aftershave while her hips moved fluidly to the next song. She pushed her way out of another group of dancers and fought her way to a place at the bar. She didn't know why her night turned so gloomy; she couldn't even have fun at the club. Money was what she had always wanted after growing up at an orphanage and becoming friends with one of the richest girls in the state.

"What are you drinking?" A voice asked to her left. It was a nice voice, smooth and deep, and Alina tried to persuade herself to turn and smile. To flirt with this man, pick him up, take him home, and do away with some of the loneliness that had somehow crept into her life. Instead, she found herself pushing away from the bar.

"Sorry." She muttered and lost herself in the sea of dancing people until she somehow made it to the door. She waited for her driver by the curb of the club, her coat missing somewhere inside, and her without a care for it. She was freezing by the time he finally pulled up, all the sweat she worked up dancing seemed to have frozen on her body. She was shocked to learn it was past midnight, but the numbers glared at her from the dash of her private car. Going to a club always seemed like stepping into a portal to her, you'd swear you were only there for twenty minutes, but it turns out to be four hours instead.

"Thanks, Paul." She said when they got to her building and with an amazing act of sobriety, she managed to not only make it inside but up into her floor. She wasted no time stripping naked and falling into her bed. *I'll just take a shower before I go to meet Simon tomorrow,* was her last thought before she fell into a dead sleep.

CHAPTER TWO

That morning Alina woke naked and alone in her bed, almost twenty minutes late for her meeting with Simon Aldridge. She groaned and let her face fall back into her pillow. *Why was it I thought going clubbing would be a good idea?* Her skull throbbed in time with each beat of her heart, her stomach churning as she groaned again. *I'm getting too old to go clubbing. When you hit thirty, someone should warn you the hangovers get worse.* She pushed herself up off the bed and shuffled into her bathroom, the hardwood floor like ice on her bare feet.

She stood under the warm spray; face tilted towards the water until the warmth started to chill. Once it started to lose its steam, she quickly scrubbed and washed her hair, pinning the long, dark strands up so she could dry off. When she was finally ready for her meeting, dressed in a formfitting pencil skirt and black and white blouse. She left her hair down in dark waves that fell to frame her face. It may not have been very professional but once someone hits a billion-net worth, people start making exceptions. Thankfully, the perks of living in a downtown penthouse were that you already were downtown. She didn't need to take her driver to take her to the modern office building next to the labs where Simon worked, she could easily and quickly walk the distance. Another plus, the rain from yesterday assured that the sidewalks were relatively empty.

Her heels clicked on the polished floor as she glanced around the busy, modern office space. Assistants and office workers hurried from desk to desk, office to office, papers, and coffee trays in hand. It was offices like this that made Alina thankful she made her fortune off the stock market and several smart investments. Just being near such a highly stressed work environment made her anxiety levels skyrocket.

She reached out and snagged the arm of an assistant she thought was named Heather. "I have a meeting with Mr. Aldridge, I'm a bit late." She said sheepishly.

"He sent out a memo to just send you up whenever you arrived." She said and ushered her to the elevator with a harried smile, her slender fingers squeezing like a vice around her elbow. Heather smiled at her a final time, friendly yet professional, as she firmly pushed her into the elevator. "Have a good day, Miss Ardelian."

"Busy day?" She asked before the elevator doors could close.

Heather smiled ruefully. "You have no idea."

The elevator doors closed between them as Alina hit the button for the top floor where Simon

Aldridge's office was located. When the doors opened, she was once again greeted by polished floors and a coldly decorated office space. Mr. Aldridge's assistant sat primly at her desk, rearranging her pens in a black tinted metal cup. She didn't bother looking up from her task as Alina approached.

"You're late." She said disinterestedly.

"I made as soon as I could." Alina said.

She nodded towards the door to his office. "Go on in, he's waiting for you."

Alina rolled her eyes, knowing she'd never see. "Thanks so much." She walked to his door, giving a quick knock before walking in and closing the door behind her.

"You're late." Simon said, sounding more amused by this than his assistant had. He stood from his long, oak-topped desk; his fingers spread across top of the beautifully wood-stained surface. Sunlight haloed around his body from the floor to ceiling windows surrounding his office. He quickly combed a few fingers through his thinning salt and pepper hair while he pinched the bottom of his, obviously tailored, ebony colored suit and tugged out an imaginary wrinkle, surveying Alina with a cheerful smile. "But that's alright. There's nothing too serious I wanted to discuss."

Alina fought to keep the polite on her face. "Then why did you call me here if there's nothing to discuss?"

"I wanted to tell you in person that we've finished the exhibit and as you already knew, our clinical study is ready to begin immediately. We open to the public on Monday, I wanted to personally invite you to the unveiling." He told her.

"Oh, well that's wonderful news but that's really something you could have mailed me in an invitation for." She said.

"I know but I really wanted to thank you again. Without your contribution this exhibit wouldn't have been possible because of you we can show the public something we all believed was lost to the world. Dragons, shifters, these were all things people had given up as fairytales and once the public loses interest, the experiments and tests we have planned could unlock the gateway to so many cures." He said fervently.

She felt goosebumps raise across her arms as she thought about standing in the presence of something supernatural, something inhuman. "Well, thanks for letting me know. I'll be at the unveiling." She assured him.

He nodded enthusiastically. "I'll get my assistant to send you the details." He rubbed his fingers across the knot of his tie, sweat beading at his temples. "I did bring some champagne if you wanted to celebrate. I know it's a little early, so I have sparkling cider too."

"Oh, I don't know-"

"I insist." He said and rushed forward to the sleek bar resting against the wall. A sweating bottle of sparkling cider sat on top of the bar in a bowl of ice. Next to it sat a glistening pitcher of water and four crystal cups, thinly sliced cucumbers floated among cubes of ice. He struggled with the cap of the cider before unscrewing the lid and gripped a short, crystal glass with a square rim and began to fill it. Alina fidgeted with the hem of her skirt as an awkward silence filled the room. She never knew what to say to Simon to make it any clearer that she wasn't interested in him. Like herself, he also found himself in a high position at a fairly young age. Being thirty herself, she had nothing against dating an older man and forty wasn't strictly what she'd call old, it was his personality that she had a problem with. Simon was always nice to her, maybe a little fervent about his studies and what his dreams for the labs were but it just became apparent after their first meeting that they had nothing in common.

He passed her a glass with trembling hands and she brought it up to her lips, taking a slow sip, and letting the cool, bubbling liquid slide down her throat and pool in the center of her belly. She averted her gaze from his eager stare and stared out the window, watching the cars pass by on the street below. There was something hypnotizing about watching others go about their day without even being aware of the people above them. She wondered if she stayed staring long enough, if he would get the hint and take a big step away from her. Probably not, the awkward silence between them only seemed to stretch the longer she kept her gaze out the window. If she studied long enough, she could see his reflection in the polished glass, his grey eyes burning holes into her back.

She brought the glass back up to her lips, quickly chugging down the contents before turning to him with a polite smile already plastered on her face. "Well, thank you for the drink. I'll see you at the unveiling." She said quickly, setting her glass on the smooth surface of his desk. Condensation slid down the crystal side and onto the expensive wood, but she inwardly shrugged, *if he ends up with glass rings, I can always buy him a new one*, she thought.

"Oh, yes, well I was wondering if you might want-"

"Don't forget to have someone sent me the details of the event." She quickly interrupted. "I'll see you Monday, Simon!" She called as she fled the office, not bothering to acknowledge his assistant as she left. The walk to the elevator and down to the main floor revealed the sound of the light pitter-patter of rain. She sighed and pulled out her phone, unwilling to walk in such poor weather. *Looks like I'll have to call my driver after all,* she thought.

***

The week passed by with a flurry of business calls and flustered messages from her accountant, she didn't even have time to meet Alicia for lunch on Saturday like she had promised. When her hard work payed off and the money started rolling in, no one warned her how much work came with such a large amount of money. Once you had it, you had to work to keep it or the expensive lifestyle that she had grown accustomed to would slowly consume the fortune.

Like Simon promised, his assistant had sent her the details for the unveiling and, despite the awkwardness she felt around Simon, Alina felt anticipation building at the bottom of her spine. She couldn't wait to see the creature they had found, to feel the power of standing in the presence of a supernatural being. The official unveiling was at four o'clock with an after-party gala for the highest donation holders and special beneficiaries such as herself. The email she received said it would be a formal event, so she was dressed to the nines in a knee length black cocktail dress and the flashiest most obnoxiously expensive jewelry she had. If she had to go to these events, she liked to make a statement. She left her hair down, curled in voluptuous, dark waves down her shoulders and back.

Her phone chimed with a text and, knowing it was her driver informing her of his arrival, she grabbed her little beaded bag and locked up for the last time tonight. She smiled thankfully as her doorman helped her into the car, she gave the driver the address to the labs and sat back in anticipation of what she would see tonight. Goosebumps raised over her arms as the air in the car seemed to electrify, a response to her nervous, excited energy. Pulling up in front of the new addition to Titan Labs that her money helped build, Alina waited until the driver came around to open the door for her.

The new building looked nothing like its older, red brick counterpart. Its newer, sleek edges and modern angles gleamed brilliantly under the glow of the spotlights the lab had set up for the occasion. She could she a few couples walking in ahead of her dressed in a similar, elegant fashion, handing their invitations to the guard stationed outside the door. She inwardly rolled her eyes. So, this was going to be a night filled with wealthy couples ogling over a creature that wouldn't even be here if it hadn't had been for her.

Just lovely, she thought.

"Invitation, please." The guard drawled, obviously bored and in for a long night.

"I don't need an invitation. My name is Alina Ardelian." She told him and saw the recognition flash in his eyes.

"Please, go right on in, Miss Ardelian. Mr. Aldridge has a private, elevated viewing platform right up the stairs to the left." He told her in a rush.

"Thank you." She said and allowed him to open the door for her while she entered. This was the first time she had seen the new building in person. She declined all of Simon's earlier invitations because she wanted the first time she saw the building to also be the first time she saw the supernatural creature that it held. It was as cold and sterile as she had imagined, all luxurious and five-star for the beneficiaries benefit tonight, but she could see the darkened doorway in the corner and the room lined with shelves beyond it. *A gift shop for the masses,* she thought dryly.

The bottom floor was quickly filling up with people, so much so that she couldn't see through the row of heads peering through the thick glass into the exhibit. *Thank goodness for Simon and his private viewing area,* she thought. She was getting impatient as she made her way to one of the two stairs that lead to the elevated platform. Simon had guards posted here too, turning away anyone who wasn't on their list. *Must only be for the high spenders.* She could practically feel the energy crackling in the room, just as she had all those years ago when she felt something watching her in her college apartment. The feeling was just as addictive as it was before, she had to get closer, she had to see it.

She moved past the guards with a mention of her name and climbed the steps like a woman in a dream. She could see Simon coming towards her, two glasses of champagne clutched in his hands, his lips moving. She couldn't hear the words he spoke to her, her hands clutched the railing of the viewing platform, her body leaning precariously over the edge as she looked down into the exhibit for the first time. Gray stone rose to meet her.

Directly opposite of her, the wall looked like

it had been pulled out of a cave and transplanted here. Gray stone, all the walls were lined with it. It didn't look fake. Below, pine and fir trees rose from the gray stone and dirt, a stream curved its way between them, allowing the creature fresh water. She tried to focus her gaze, staring desperately to try and find the creature. *How hard can it be to find a dragon in a cage?* She thought impatiently, but the size of the exhibit had shocked her. She knew it would have to be big if they were housing a dragon, but it looked like they had transplanted a small forest into the center of the laboratory.

The air crackled with energy around her as she finally laid eyes on it. *Not it,* her mind corrected, *him.* He was standing directly in the center of the exhibit, his piercing green eyes staring straight up at her. The next thing she noticed was the thick lank of hair that hung down around his face. It was red, not ginger but deep, burgundy, thick and rich like a good wine. His eyes, forest green, the color of the tips of the pine, had not left hers. It also hadn't escaped her notice that he was shirtless. Thick cords of muscle stretched across his back and shoulders, biceps fluttering as he tensed and relaxed his stance. His chest was smooth, a light dusting of hair leading to the hard ridges of his abs and dipping inside the loose jeans he wore.

His gaze jerked away from her, staring straight ahead, seemingly into the crowd of spectators below. A jet of steam erupted from his nostrils as he began to pace. It didn't take a genius to see he was getting agitated. In a fit of anger, Alina watched as he began to transform. The size of his body seemed to double then triple as scales the same rich burgundy of his hair began to cover his skin. It happened quickly, one moment a beautiful man stood in the center of a glorified cage and within the next several blinks of an eye there was a tall, handsome dragon in his place. His scales shimmered under the glaring spotlights, fiery red and outlined with black. It wasn't the kind of dragon she had ever seen in movies, this one stood tall, its snake-like, twisting neck leading up to the thick head and curling black horns. He opened his mouth and a quick, forked tongue darted out in a hiss directed towards the people down front.

She could feel Simon's sweaty hands tugging at her elbow, trying to pull her back but her attention was solely focused on the thing below. The dragon took a step back and suddenly massive wings were arching away from his back in an aggressive gesture. Another hiss, the forked tongue flicking angrily before a jet of liquid flames burst from the dragon's mouth and hit the reinforced window filled with peering faces. The crowd jumped, one woman screamed, but the rest were clapping like he was some zoo animal performing a trick. In a wave of fury, he took to the sky, flying in small circle around his enclosed exhibit and blasting the glass surrounding him with his deadly fire.

Alina could feel a wave of heat sweep over her even though the glass protected her from the flames. She finally spared a glance at Simon but found his attention no longer on her. Instead, he was staring eagerly into the exhibit as the man turned dragon circled his prison, spraying fire in useless, erratic bursts. She could feel the power thrumming from this man, the supernatural energy that crackled between them, but instead of soothing the addiction she gained in college, she felt like she had destroyed it. Everything she had worked for; every seedy deal and underhanded investment had been led by the frantic search for power money. It didn't feel like it had before, there was no satisfaction, it tasted like ashes in her mouth. She had found what she wanted, fame, recognition, and at what cost? A man's life? His freedom?

***

Hours later, Alina found herself in the ballroom Simon had rented for the evening. It was so luxurious it almost made her sick. Polished red oak floors stretched under her heels and expensive fairy lights floated around her, hung up around the bar. Her too big bed and a large cheese pizza had never sounded better than when she glanced over the trays of tiny, unrecognizable foods she'd be forced to dine on that night.

At least she had been able to slip away from Simon after the end of the "show" that the shifter put on. Other guests that she thought she might know all vied for a piece of her attention. It also seemed like she was one of the few here without a date because with every couple that snagged her arm, came the question of her relationship status, her lack of a date, and more specifically, her lack of husband. She'd like to know if every woman had to deal with this once they turned thirty or if it was just eligible billionaires and heiresses.

She was stuck here for at least an hour, so she could establish a presence before she could leave and figure out what she was going to do. She couldn't live with herself if she left that poor man to live his life out within the exhibit and worse, to be experimented on in the labs just out of the public's eyes. She sighed and pushed the thought from her mind. She couldn't worry about it here; she had an image to maintain. She had to at least pretend she was enjoying herself; she didn't want anyone thinking that she looked suspicious. Even though it would be hard to enjoy herself when her loyal friend Alicia wouldn't be here to rescue her from being sober, single, and possibly plotting a rescue mission. Alicia's boyfriend, who worked several states away, had surprised her for the night, and they would both be lost to each other until morning.

Finally, Alina lost her army of followers and made it to the bar. She slid onto a stool, prepared for a long evening of drinking and dodging anyone looking for conversation.

"What can I get you?" The bartender asked. She

was a middle-aged woman with a kind face and a sympathetic look in her eyes.

"Wine, whatever the house wine is please." She requested, in no state of mind to comprehend the long wine list stretched out in front of her and even longer list of beers on tap. She downed the first glass almost as soon as she placed it on a coaster and the bartender shot her another sympathetic glance, wordlessly pouring her a fresh one. She turned to rest her back on the bar, unable to take the sympathy any longer. All these years and a billion dollars later and she was still a creature that was pitied. She watched as a second bartender handed over a round of mixed drinks to a group of laughing guests a few stools down the bar. How could they be so happy after what they had just seen? *Were we even seeing the same thing? A man trapped in his own personal hell. Looking forward to a life of captivity, stares, and whatever experiments awaited him?*

They eventually left the bar, taking their drinks and heading towards one of the tables filled with expensive, disgusting food. Alina sighed and leaned back against the bar.

"Another?" A voice asked. "Miss, would you like another?"

"Sorry." She muttered. "Yes, I would, please."

She could hear the pop as the bartender opened another bottle of wine, the soft trickle as it was poured into her glass. "Here you are." She said and cast another sympathetic glance at her, making

Alina want to roll her eyes. Instead, she nodded her thanks took a huge gulp of her new glass. She had never needed alcohol more. Something in the crowd caught her eye, coming towards her and looking determined, was Simon.

CHAPTER THREE

The short, prematurely balding man was wearing a spotless, perfectly tailored black tux and shiny, polished black shoes. Alina narrowed her eyes slightly, swirling the wine in her glass in a small circle. "Hello, Simon." She inwardly sighed. *My evening just got a whole lot worse.*

Simon stirred his own drink with a little plastic straw, the ice cubes clinking around in the glass. "Alina! Wasn't that the most thrilling thing you've ever seen? I imagine this will be one of the biggest tourist destinations within the month. All proceeds from admissions will go to our clinical study, of course."

Alina placed her now empty glass on the bar top, another glass being poured for her before she could signal the bartender with the sympathetic face. She smiled at her in thanks and got a nod of understanding in return as she sipped her new glass. "Right, soon we'll be bigger than those pandas they make breed at the zoo." She said, unable to control the loathing and sarcasm in her voice. Simon looked shocked for a moment.

"Alina-I mean-Miss Ardelian, I don't understand. The audience's reception of this creature was more than we had ever dreamed to hope. We're nothing like a zoo. The research we're going to conduct on this creature could save the lives of millions." He told her, somewhat cautiously this time.

The multicolor spotlights that had been beaming over the dance floor changed to a brilliant mix of blues, pinks, and white, the size of the lights reminiscent of club laser beams and instantly changing the atmosphere of the room. Guests began to drift from the food over to the dance floor, smiles on their faces and absolutely no regard for the man in a glorified cage the next room over. Lifting her wine glass, Alina became aware of the awkward tension rising between her and Simon. She still hadn't responded to him and observed as he nervously sucked the end of the stirrer into his mouth, a small drop of alcohol or mixer glistening on his lips. He did what he thought was a discreet sweep of her body, but she caught it, saw the way his eyes lingered on her hips and breasts.

She'd had enough of Simon, of these people, and this sickening event. She didn't care if she looked suspicious or rude. She shot him a withering glare and finished her wine, grabbed her purse, and stormed right past him out of the building. She may not have been the one who found the shifter, but she had been the one to finance his prison and future torture. She didn't think she could sleep another night in her life it she didn't at least try to reason for his freedom with Simon. She slid into a cab and gave him the address to her building, already planning the request in her mind. She would speak to Simon first thing in the morning.

***

That morning, Alina walked into Simon Aldridge's office building with determination. Her heels clicked along the polished floor as she dodged assistants carrying piles of paperwork and trays of teas and coffees. She went right to the elevator and stabbed the button for the top floor. She did not offer Simon's assistant a polite smile or a polite anything, instead she tapped her heels against the polished floor impatiently.

"I need to see Simon, now." She demanded.

His assistant raised a perfectly manicured eyebrow. "Well, I'll have to see if he's busy."

Alina shook her head, incredulous. "Half his office is glass walls. I can see him right there. He doesn't look very busy to me." She said and motioned to where Simon sat, balling up a sheet of paper and throwing it towards his waste basket. She could see as he snuck a peek her way and sighed, running his hands through his hair. His office phone rang, and she watched with disbelief as he spared her another glance before he snatched it up. He was stalling.

His assistant looked triumphant. "Looks pretty busy to me."

"Better look again." She said, smirking inwardly

as she noticed Simon's disappointment as he said something into the phone before setting in the cradle again.

His assistant released a large sigh and stood, opening his door. "You have a visitor, sir." She said, and Simon peered out the open door like he couldn't see her through the glass.

"Ah, Miss Ardelian, please come in." He said but instead of looking eager like he usually did, he looked cautious. *He knows something's up,* she thought worriedly and followed him into his office. He had his hands shoved in his pockets. His eyes darted around before he shut the door behind her. Alina turned to the sound of Simon's assistant breaking one of the expensive vases of her desk, missing Simon jabbing a button that would call to security. When she turned around, he went back to smiling politely and tried to clear his desk of some of the paperwork while straightening his tie. She heard his desk chair squeak as he sank back into it.

"I'm afraid you caught me during a busy, busy day." He said, motioning to the paperwork as if to say look at this mess, look what I must deal with.

"Sir, the tea you ordered has arrived." His assistant said from outside his office, all professional and friendly and everything she had never been to her. Alina missed the meaningful glance she sent towards her boss.

Simon's body froze, and he clutched a bundle of papers he had picked up to move to his chest.

"That was fast." He muttered, glancing at Alina. "Tell them to wait a moment." Alina frowned, *something wasn't right,* she thought as she watched as Simon frowned down at his desk. But she wasn't one to be intimidated. She watched with satisfaction as Simon's eyes widened, his lips falling open as she strutted forward and lowered her body on the leather sofa pushed against Simon's office wall and crossed her long legs. She smirked. She knew exactly what this skirt did for her legs.

"I wanted to speak to you about the dragon shifter, what's his name?" She asked, feeling a sudden wave of guilt that she didn't even know the poor man's name.

"I believe the creature goes by the name of Darius?" He said, making it sound like a question.

She stared at him blankly. "You mean to tell me you don't know his full name? And he isn't an animal or a creature, he's a man."

His eyes widened slightly, his voice dropping to a hushed, secretive tone. "I never said he wasn't a man, and his name is Darius. I just don't think he should be considered as being totally human. Which is why it's so important, the work we're doing together. To let the world, discover and see this creature-amazing discovery for themselves. All the things we can learn, Alina! They don't get sick, you know, shifters have never had a documented case of cancer."

"I don't care! I don't feel good about this anymore. It's not right. It's not how I thought it was going to be."

Simon nodded, pasting a smile back on. "I understand how shocking last night was, Miss Ardelian, it shocked me as well. No one expected the level of power and ability that he displayed. That's why it's so wonderful that you have allowed the world to be a part of this. Without you, none of this would have been possible. I personally owe you, Miss Ardelian."

She was shaking her head. "No, I don't think you're understanding what I'm saying, Simon-"

"Just this morning alone we've gotten more funding for the lab through admission tickets than we have in a year's donations!" He continued fervently.

"No, Simon, I don't want to be a part of this anymore. We need to get Darius out, we need to get him home-"

"So exciting, imagine what our numbers will be for a year." He said and gripped her tightly by the arm. She was met at the door by one of the buildings security guards. "It was wonderful seeing you, Miss Ardelian." He said and closed the door in her face.

***

That night, standing outside the darkened building of the lab, Alina felt something heavy sinking into the pit of her stomach, making her lips turn down into a frown. *I'm so stupid, of course they'd have guards posted. Simon would never leave someone as valuable as Darius unguarded.* She ducked behind the corner of the building again. When she had returned home after her failed attempt at talking to Simon she had decided to try and handle the situation by herself. Meaning, she had gone home and planned a jail break. She wasn't entirely sure how she'd get Darius across the ocean and to his homeland once she had him out but with the amount of money at her fingertips, she was sure she could figure something out. But first she'd have to figure out how to get past the guards.

She decided on the direct approach. "Hi, would you mind unlocking the door for me?" She asked as she approached the guard with all the confidence she could muster. Sometimes you could get people to let you in as long as they believed you really belonged there. "I'm sure Simon gave you my name. Alina Ardelian."

The guard did not look impressed. "Mr. Aldridge gave me strict orders. No one goes in that building until six."

"I'm guessing fifty thousand dollars would change your mind?" She asked, and the guard had the door open before she could finish writing the check. "If you double cross me, I'll call my bank and have this canceled." She warned but the man was already shaking his head.

"Don't worry about me, I've always wanted to move to California." He told her, staring at the amount of money that barely fit in the little amount column on the check.

"Good, go tonight." She said and entered the darkened building without a single look back. When the door shut behind her, she was pitched into sudden and absolute darkness. "Damn, I really should have brought a flashlight." She said into the dark. She fumbled along the wall for a light switch before realizing that was useless and then began navigating the empty lab via the glow of her smartphone. "Hey, there's a flashlight app!"

She spent longer than she anticipated fumbling around in the dark and when she did finally find the door that led to Darius's enclosure, she found it locked. "Of course, it's locked." She mumbled to herself. "Did you expect to just walk right in, take him by the hand, and walk right back out?" She scolded herself for poor planning and spent the next hour wandering around the dark building, looking for a key. She finally found one in the janitor's cupboard of all places and gripped it tight with a triumphant "Aha!"

She hesitated before she unlocked the door, knowing that while this man needed her help, he was also extremely dangerous. She could be opening this door and walking right to her death. She shook her head, mentally preparing herself. "It's a risk I'll just have to take." She told herself, not wanting to admit that this wasn't the first time she had resorted to talking to herself and unlocked the door. She stepped inside the enclosure, her shoes scraping against the gray stone under her feet. Somehow, it wasn't as dark inside the exhibit, they must have put a few dim lights in here, so Darius could see at night.

"Darius?" She called softly, peering through the trees as she tried to catch a glimpse of him. "You don't know me, but my name is Alina and I came to get you out. To get you home." She continued.

"I do know you." He said, suddenly standing before her. His voice was rough and heavily accented, a mix of English and Eastern European. "I saw you last night." His handsome face twisted in a sneer as he jerked his head towards the viewing area. "Up there." He was still shirtless, his skin smooth and glowing in the dim light of the enclosure. His hair hung down the sides of his face, a natural curl at the ends. His expression the picture of wary, his posture towards her tense but the vibrant green eyes and deep rose lips, were even more radiant in the soft lighting of night than they had been the previous evening during the unveiling.

"I was up there but I'm not like the others, Darius. I didn't realize-I just came here to make things right, okay? To get you out and bring you home." She said. "I swear, I'm going to get you out of here, but you have to trust me." She tried not to shiver as familiar energy began to crackle between them as he stepped closer. Her breath caught as he came to a stop right in front of her and Darius ducked down, smoothly moving his face to the crook neck, taking a slow, long sniff. Alina's body was frozen in place, she didn't dare move while the tip of his nose brushed against the soft skin of her neck.

Darius stepped closer to her then, his body heat moving into hers, making her face flush. She felt attraction flowing through her, building as he ran his fingertips over the tops of her hands, tracing her knuckles with his calloused fingertips, angling his body towards her own. She felt his lips purse to place small, light, barely-there kiss along the side of her neck, before he was pulling away from her. She swallowed as he did, her throat suddenly dry, and her pulse pounding faster and faster.

"No, you are not like them." He finally said.

Alina swallowed; the back of her throat thick. "What were you doing?"

"Questions would be best saved for later. You said you were here to get me out of this place?" He asked, the roughness of his voice making goosebumps rise on her arms.

"Yes, um, I'm Alina, by the way." She said, and he tipped his head down at her in acknowledgement, bringing her hand up to kiss.

"And how, Alina, will you be getting us out?" He asked.

"Right through the front door." She said. "But first we need to make it look like you broke out of here on your own. If I showed you the hidden door in here that leads to the rest of the lab, could you break it down?" She asked and was shocked by his booming laugh in return.

"I've been searching for such a door to do just

that, but to no avail." He said and motioned her to lead him. She showed him the hidden door she had entered from and watched with amazement and maybe a little bit of fear as he broke through it effortlessly.

"Jeez, no wonder they camouflaged that so well. You're awfully expensive to contain." She said but wilted at his unimpressed stare. "Too soon?" Several minutes later, she felt like a complete ass for joking about his containment after watching him inhale the fresh air with his head tilted back towards the stars.

"I have not seen the night's sky in far longer than I want to admit." He told her, but she was busy glancing around the empty street.

"I'm so sorry but we really do need to get out of sight and back to my apartment. You walking around, shirtless, looking like some kind of god is just a little bit too conspicuous for my tastes." She said.

A frown was instantly on his face, twisting his handsome features. "Your apartment? You said you were taking me home." His tone was accusing.

"I know I did, and I am!" She snapped. "But everyone in the world will be looking for you by morning. You need somewhere to hide out until I can think of a way to smuggle you out of the country."

He studied her for a moment before making his decision. "Alright, I will trust you. Take me to this apartment."

***

So, having a dragon shifter hiding out in her apartment might have been a spur of the moment and, now that she had time to see him standing outside her building as she tried to think of a way to get them both up unseen by the doorman, generally bad idea. Suddenly remembering that her building had a rear entrance, she grabbed Darius's thick wrist, dragging him around to the back of the building. The burly, balding security guard on duty stared at her long and hard, with a knowing smirk planted on his face as he studied the pair of them. *Oh, the picture we must make,* she thought. Darius stood blinking at him, maintaining his aggressive stance while his eyes flicked back and forth between Alina and the other man, he obviously didn't know whether or not to attack. Their staring contest went on for nearly half a minute, tension and rigid muscles on Darius's side, a knowing smirk on the guard's. Finally, the guard eventually lifted a telephone from his desk, punching a few digits into the glowing keypad.

The guard said nothing but pressed a button on his right, embedded in the bricks. There was a single beep and then he was swinging the doors open for them. "First elevator to right, goes straight up, Miss Ardelian."

Alina nodded, a warm blush on her cheeks. "Thank you." She said quickly and moved to pull Darius inside, hesitating only for a moment. "Um, and I'd appreciate your discretion."

He winked, leering briefly at them. "All in my job description, Miss Ardelian."

She nodded her thanks went straight to the elevator and stepped into the first one, pressing the top button for the floor of her penthouse. She almost forgot about Darius, who was standing outside, looking puzzled at the elevator. She sighed heavily and reached out, dragging him in before the doors could shut and the elevator started to rise quietly. They stood together in silence, Alina watching the numbers light and fade as they passed each floor.

"Are we traveling up the building?" Darius finally asked as their neared the end of their ascent.

"Yeah, I live on the top floor." She said.

"It would have been faster to fly." He pointed out.

"Yes, but I can't fly so, you know, elevators." She finished lamely. He looked surprised by her answer but before he could say anything else the doors pinged open. She pulled him out of the elevator and into the short hall where her door stood. She had never been so relieved to be home. She dug her keys out and opened the door for him. "Welcome to your home for the next few weeks. I have a couple spare rooms, so you can pick which one you like the best." She rambled as she led him inside, shutting and bolting the door behind them. "Are you hungry?" She asked, and he looked down at her with what she would classify as a smile, but it looked a bit on the predatory side.

"You may bring food if you wish. I believe we have much to discuss." He said.

"Right." She said. "Well, I'll just go get something from the kitchen. You can explore or whatever."

When she came back, carrying a plate of assorted snacks, she saw he had taken her advice and was exploring his new surroundings. She smiled softly at the sight of him touching the bottom corner of some painting she had paid a ridiculous amount of money for and tilting it down until all the edges were even. She didn't have the heart to tell him it was meant to hang crooked. For a fearsome creature, he could look incredibly adorable at times.

She cleared her throat. "I brought food."

He turned and smiled at her, the first true smile she had seen from him. "Good. We will eat and then we will talk." He said and took long strides across the thick carpet. With a jolt she realized that he was barefoot and had been barefoot this entire time. *I made him walk an entire city block like this,* she thought, *I'll have to check and make sure he didn't cut his feet on anything.* Alina came up next to him, meeting him halfway across the carpet. He didn't lay a finger on her, but his body seemed to produce vibrations of energy, a heated power that moved between him and her and left the air crackling.

Alina found that her voice was a whisper, her

hands clutching tight to the ceramic plate she held. "What is this? This energy between us? You have to feel it to."

Darius chuckled softly; his voice was rough but felt like satin across her skin. "Do you really not know? You and I aren't so different, Alina. We share a little blood between us."

"What do you mean? Are you saying we're related?" She asked.

"Yes and no, we share some blood but yours is diluted, weak. I doubt any of our forebears crossed paths within the last few hundred years." He said but Alina could hardly comprehend what he was saying. Who used words like forebears anyway? This situation was officially too crazy even for her, who had experienced her fair share of crazy before.

"So, you're telling me I'm a dragon shifter?"

CHAPTER FOUR

Darius's deep, booming laugh filled the empty spaces of her apartment. "You, a shifter? No, maybe your ancestors, a thousand years ago, but not you."

"So, my ancestors were like you?" She asked, not sure whether to be relieved or not by what he was telling her. *Hey, turning into a huge, fire-breathing dragon could have been handy,* she thought.

"Yes, I could tell the moment I laid eyes on you." He said.

"So that's why you were staring at me!" She exclaimed, and Darius almost looked sheepish.

"I apologize for that." He muttered.

"And was that why you were smelling me?" She pressed.

Now he really did look uncomfortable. "...Yes."

"So, is that why I have-I don't really know if you can call it a power-but is that why I can feel energies sometimes?" She asked.

"Yes, you may not be a shifter, but you can feel when you are in the presence of the supernatural." He explained.

Alina sat down hard on her leather sofa, Darius

reaching out to steady her. "No, I'm all right. This is just a lot to take in for one day, especially considering today I also committed my first major crime." She took a deep breath. "Where is your home? Where did they find you, Darius, and why did you go with them?"

"Noregr," he told her, his voice was low and rough. "But you would call it Norway. I was hiding in a cave when they found me, the researchers. They had seen me change, I guess, but they didn't give me any chance to explain myself. They shot me with something, it made me dizzy, weak, and I couldn't shift. I collapsed. When I woke, I was in a cage, they kept me weak, so I couldn't change, and, in a few weeks, I woke up in the enclosure. No one would listen to a word I said. You were the first."

"That's terrible, Darius. I am so sorry for what happened to you." She said and gripped his hand, her fingers brushing over his knuckles. "I promise I'll get you back to your homeland."

"But not yet?" He asked.

"Not yet. I can probably bribe a ship to get you home, but we need to wait until the search for you calms down. By morning, every news crew in the world will be reporting your escape." She said.

"But I did not escape, you rescued me." He said.

"That's why we made it look like you busted out." She explained and suddenly remembered the plate she held in her hands. "Oh, I almost forgot. Here, take this and eat all of it. You've got to be starving, it doesn't look like they were feeding you much."

"No, they weren't." He agreed and took the plate when she handed it to him. He ate the cheese slices first, then the sad couple of grapes she had found in the bottom of her vegetable crisper. He hesitated at the other snacks. "I'm not sure what these are."

"Oh, that's Nutella. Just eat it with a spoon, I do but then I get scolded by my trainer." She confessed and watched eagerly as he took a spoonful. He coughed, and she erupted into giggles. "Not to your taste?"

"No, it's good. It sticks to the mouth though." He said and put the spoon back on the tray.

She smiled at him fondly before shaking her head. "Okay, no more Nutella. Come on, it's very, very late and I know I'm exhausted, so you must be too. I'll show you too the spare rooms, you can pick which one you want."

She led him down the hall, following the same dark hardwood floor that ran through her apartment. She showed him the first guest room, the large, king-sized bed was fitted with all white sheets, a white comforter, and four fluffy white pillows. She winced at the sterile feel of at all but at least there was a flat screen mounted to the wall in front of the bed. Darius smiled, the twist of his lips slow, but his smile easy. He looked sheepish, running his fingers through the back of his tangled hair.

"Thank you." He said, and they locked eyes. Much softer, he said to her, "Alina," he swallowed, "thank you." They stared at each other, Alina's breast heaving visibly beneath the thin cloth covering her chest. Darius' eyes traced the flushed skin spreading from her face down her neck and visibly swallowed.

"You're welcome," Alina finally said, and Darius let his gaze slip down Alina's body and back up again, his eyes blazing hot yet still gentle.

"Right. I, um. Goodnight, I guess." Alina chuckled breathlessly before hanging her head and backpedaling rapidly out of the room.

Darius nodded slowly, his eyes never leaving her face. "Goodnight, Alina." Alina let out another breathless sound and turned away, glancing over her shoulder to find Darius still staring at her, his expression could only be described as smoldering.

She fled quickly down the hall and to her own bed, standing on the end, she spread out her arms, closed her eyes, and belly flopped into her nest of pillows, letting out a groan. She rolled over onto her side, clutching a pillow to her chest. "Why does he have to be hot?" She asked herself. She contemplated smothering herself with the pillow to avoid further embarrassment, but decided against it, instead going into her bathroom to take care of her bedtime ritual. She rid herself of her clothes and crawled into bed, taking a deep breath, and staring up at the ceiling.

"Okay. Time to sleep. Go to sleep." She shut her eyes and wiggled deeper under the silky covers.

From that second on, every small sound she heard had her eyes snapping open, her body tossing and turning in bed as she thought of Darius only a room away.

"Oh, come on. Get over it, Alina. That man is a God and whatever you're feeling is obviously one-sided, brought on by one too many fantasies and delusions." She sighed after her little pep talk and turned onto her stomach, falling into a light sleep.

***

Alina was rinsing the teapot from her morning cup and was placing it in a drying rack when the door opened, and the muffled shuffle of feet across the carpet alerted her to the presence of her guest. She smiled at Darius from the sink, drying her hands on a dish towel. She faltered when he walked towards her, caging her body against the counter. His hair was freshly washed and smelled like the clean, fresh scented shampoo she kept stocked in the guest bedroom. He reached past her to grab one of the drying mugs, ducking his head to rub his cheek against hers in a subtle brush, his slight stubble rough on Alina's skin.

"Morning," Darius said. "Do you mind if I make some?" His half-lidded eyes landed on Alina's lips. "I've missed having something hot in the mornings."

Alina chewed nervously on the corner of her lip before ignoring every part of her brain screaming that this was a bad idea and lifted herself on the balls of her feet as he ducked down, their lips softly meeting in the middle. A fizzle of something electric traveled up her spine during the kiss, making all the hairs on the back of her neck stand up. Their lips remained pressed together, closed but firm. They caught eyes and Alina found herself hypnotized in the deep, forest green abyss until her eyes fluttered closed and she lost herself in the kiss, their bodies pressing closer. Darius's hand molded around Alina's hip, his other hand lifting to entangle in her hair.

Alina wilted against him, their lips softly sucking together. Alina's back bumped into the counter as Darius pulled away from her mouth, kissing the corner of her lips. Alina's head tilted to bring their lips together again, Darius exhaling a hot breath out of his nostrils, the steam rising between them. With their lips tenderly pressed together, Alina let out a soft whimper and let his thigh nudge her legs open. Darius's palm slid down the smooth, sensitive skin of her lower back and when it reached her ass, his hand curled around the plump mound of her right cheek. Alina made a louder, whimpering moan, and arched her hips so she could get some friction from his thigh.

Then Darius's heat was suddenly gone. "I shouldn't have…" Darius said, trailing off. He was flattened against the opposite counter.

Alina blinked, wide eyed. "You should really get out of the habit of assuming you know what a woman wants. Trust me, if I didn't want you to kiss me, you would have heard about it."

Darius kept his eyes politely on Alina's face rather than her heaving breast and her still opened legs. "You rescued me from that hell and sheltered me in your home. Taking advantage of you is hardly the payment I should offer."

"If anything, I'm taking advantage of you. You're the one stuck in my apartment. So, shut up and let me take advantage of you. I want this, want you. I've wanted it since I first saw you in that display and-" Darius tilted his head and firmly pressed his lips to Alina's mouth, silencing her rant. Their eyes were locked and unblinking. Alina pulled back an inch, Darius's mouth meeting air. Darius gripped Alina's hips and pulled her tightly into his body, the pull hard enough for Alina's lips to connect with his again.

"All right," Darius murmured, his hand snaking up to massage her breast. "Then take advantage of me." He leaned in, brushing a kiss to her pulse point. He opened his teeth on the spot, her throat bobbing as he licked and bit at her neck. Alina took his face in both hands and guided him up. Inexplicable heat, like the spark from a fire or a lightning storm, jolted between them as his mouth was pried open by Alina's wet, confident tongue. Their teeth clashed together as waves of heat pulsed through Alina's thin shirt, their shifting causing it to ride up on her stomach. Darius hitched her shirt up, his hot palm burning with each squeeze against her breast.

When she tried to pull back, tried to break

their marathon of kisses, her body refused to listen, save for an involuntary grind against his thick thigh between her legs. The sure motions of his lips and hands made Alina feel like they were the only people left on the earth. Everything narrowed down to the two of them. They were inches away from another kiss when Alina surged forward, nipping at his lower lip. She cradled the back of his head then and guided Darius's head towards her breast. Alina sighed high in a voice and hugged Darius closer with her thighs, as Darius swiped his tongue over her cloth covered nipple, sucking, and nibbling until Alina trembled under him.

He pulled away from her chest and whispered against her parted lips. "Touch me." Her eyes followed the motion of his long fingers as he popped each button of the night shirt he had found. The shirt fluttered open, the cotton material framing his muscled torso. Darius guided her hand over the hard ridges of his abs. He looked like someone who worked the land all day, chopping wood and tending the soil, his body lean and muscled without being overly so like some of the gym rats that often stalked Alina in the clubs. Darius shrugged his shoulders back, his shirt melting down his strong shoulders and back, fluttering to the kitchen tile, "you can touch me as much as you like."

The shrill ring of Alina's cell sliced through the heavy air between them. It rang three times before Alina shifted awkwardly against him. "Um, I should probably see who that is."

"Of course, forgive me." Darius said and released her from the prison of his arms. She saw him quickly grab a glass of water and chug it, something that looked suspiciously like steam billowing from his open lips as he drank before she darted for her phone.

She groaned as she read the name on her screen, swiping her thumb across it to answer. "Has anyone ever told you that you have the worst fucking timing on earth?"

Alicia's high-pitched laugh tinkled out her phone like bell chimes. "What? Don't tell me you let Simon take you home. Is he freaking out? Wait, if he's with you then does he even know yet?"

"Don't be vulgar, of course I didn't let him take me home. Now, what are you talking about?"

"Shit, you really don't know. I'm surprised no one's called you. That lab project you've been sponsoring, apparently the thing escaped last night. It's all over the news." Alicia told her.

"He's not a thing-shit." Alina closed her eyes, cursing herself over the slip.

"Oh, Alina, don't tell me... Don't tell me. It's better if I don't know. Come meet me for lunch. It'll be more suspicious if you just keep holed up in your apartment. One o'clock at Lela's?"

"I really don't-"

"Alina, if you suddenly drop off the map they're going to come looking."

"No, no, you're right. I'll meet you there. I might

have a favor to ask anyway." Alina said.

"See you soon, don't commit anymore felonies before we meet!"

"Can't promise anything. See you at one, Ali. Bye." Alina set her phone on the counter. She gave a quick reassuring smile to Darius who was staring at her phone warily. "Don't worry, everything is fine. I just need to meet a friend soon. You'll be okay on your own, won't you? I have some books; I don't really know what you like to read. Mine are mostly romance but I think I have some of my old college textbooks, although, I don't know why I thought you'd want to read that-"

"Alina, Alina," he interrupted. "I will be perfectly content to wait for you and when you return, we can speak further."

"Speak...right. Actually, we should really talk soon." She said, smiling softly. "I want to hear about your life in Norway and I have questions about...well, everything."

******

It was raining when Alina got to Lela's Cafe, her coat tucked over her head as a makeshift umbrella. She pulled the door open and nearly bumped someone standing in the front of the busy restaurant. "You know, I know for a fact you own like twenty umbrellas, but I've never actually seen you use one." Alicia said.

"Ha-ha, very funny, it didn't look like it was going to rain." Alina said as they walked further inside together. She shrugged her wet coat off, hanging it on the rack beside the door and said to the hostess, "two for lunch, please."

"Right this way." The hostess said, smiling and gesturing with two menus in hand. They followed her down a narrow aisle of crowded tables until they were seated next to a window, rain sliding down the glass. The waitress filled their glasses with water as the two women browsed the menus, cautious of what they might say while in the presence of listening ears.

"Have you two decided?" she chirped, looking from Alina to Alicia. "Or I could start you with something to drink?"

"I'd like a glass of the house white, please." Alina said. "Actually, you know what? Just bring the whole bottle."

"Excellent choice." The waitress murmured, scribbling on her notepad.

"Then," Alina continued, "we'll have the quiche of the day, no soup, no salad, just the quiche." She shot her a quick smile before dismissing her with a thank you.

"Wow, someone's in a hurry." Alicia said, giving her friend a strange look.

"I get what you mean about people needing to see me out in the public eye or whatever but that doesn't mean I'm going to take a three-hour lunch." She hissed quietly.

"Oh my God, you actually-so you did-Holy shit, Alina!" Alicia hissed back; shock clear on her face. "You could go to prison for this, I don't think that even *you* could buy your way out of this one."

"That's why I need your help, okay? I need to get out of the country but not in a flashy, take my own private jet kind of way. I need something low key." She looked at her meaningfully.

"You mean you want me to get you and a friend on one of my dad's boats, am I right?"

Alina looked down at the tablecloth guiltily. "I would never drag you or your family into this if I had any other options."

Alicia sighed. "I know... Look, I can get you on a boat but my dad ships *steel*. It's not exactly going to be a luxury cruise."

"I don't care about any of that. I'd sleep on a bed of coal, just get us out of here." Alina begged, falling silent as the waitress came back to their table. She poured them each a glass of wine, leaving the bottle as she went to retrieve their meal.

"Where do you need to go?" Alicia asked, already tapping rapid texts out on her phone.

"Norway, or as close as you can get us to it. And we need to leave sooner rather than later." Alina said, taking long sips of her wine and thanking the waitress when she returned with their food.

"Well, I can't do Norway, but I can get you to Cork, Ireland. Ship leaves tomorrow." She said.

Alina thought it over while chewing on a bite of quiche. "I'll take it."

"Okay, then I'll meet you in the shipyard tomorrow at 6 AM. Do not be late." She shook her head. "I hope you know what you're doing. Is it even worth it? If you turn it in now maybe-"

"He's not an it, Alicia, don't call him that. It is worth it; I think this might be the most important thing I ever do in my life." Alina said.

Alicia watched her friend knowingly, a small smile on her lips. "Yeah, okay. I see what this is about. You'll text me when the eggs hatch, right?"

Alina kicked her in the shin, delighting in the indignant squawk that escaped her mouth. "You aren't funny."

"No, seriously though, are you going to have babies or eggs with your lovebird?"

"Shut up!"

"Oh my God, you don't even know, do you?"

"I said shut up."

CHAPTER FIVE

Alina returned to her apartment after the first hour of her lunch began to trickle into the second. Thoughts of Darius consumed her mind even while she was talking and joking with her friend. She didn't understand how she could be so attached to a man that she had just met, but just because she didn't understand it, didn't mean it wasn't real. She was prepared to leave her entire world behind for him, but she couldn't deny the bond that had somehow cemented between them.

When the elevators slid open, Alina was met with the sight of Darius, towel slung low on his hips and a puzzled frown on his lips as he stared hard at the T.V. "Oh, oh no, are you really watching Downton Abbey?"

"It was...on." He said.

"I thought you were going to get more dressed. You're less dressed." She pointed out, setting her purse on a nearby end table.

He shrugged; his attention recaptured by the television set. "I am not used to wearing clothes."

"Right..." She said, clicking the T.V. off and ignoring the pout that should have looked ridiculous on a grown man. "I managed to find us a boat. It won't take us to Norway, but it will get us out of the country."

"How far?" He asked.

"Ireland. Cork, if I'm remembering right." She answered.

He beamed then, looking the happiest she had ever seen him. "I have cousins in Ireland!"

"Really?"

"The Vikings made many trips to Ireland." He said, shrugging one of his shoulders. "Some of my ancestors tagged along."

"Ancestors, right. So, by cousins you mean people who are very distantly related to you that you have never met?"

"Correct."

"Perfect." She said with a little sigh.

The smile slipped from Darius's face. "Alina, you don't owe me anything. I would not ask you to sacrifice your entire life. Just being free is a gift enough."

"No, it's not-" she made a soft, frustrated sound. "I'm not upset about leaving this all behind. I guess...It just scares me how easy it feels. I want to go with you."

He walked forward then, his large, warm hands cupping each side of her face. "Only if you are sure because I meant it. You don't have to do anything you don't want to."

"When will you learn?" She laughed softly as his eyes searched hers, confused by her mirth. "I *never* do anything I don't want to." She surged up to her toes, melding their lips together. The kiss shared between them was full of heat, tongues exploring, and teeth catching on lips. She reached down, yanking the towel away from his hips. She pressed her palms against the hard planes of his chest until he took a step back, allowing her to admire his cock, long and heavy as it filled.

Warmth pooled in her belly as she drug her eyes back up his muscled torso to his face. His eyes were dark, and he dipped his head just as she stepped forward to press her body against his. His lips felt a rough against hers, their tongues returning to their former battle. She could feel his cock rise against her fabric clad thigh as one of his hands drifted towards her ass, kneading the flesh as the other hand pushed between them, deft fingers slipping under her shirt and the cup of her bra to tweak her nipple.

Soon the sound of her moans echoed off the walls of the living room as she rocked her hips against his. "I would take you in your bed, at least the first time." He spoke the words against her lips as he lifted her up, her legs wrapping instantaneously around his hips. He carried her into her bedroom, falling over her against the soft, silk sheets. "Are you very attached to this blouse?"

She shook her head. "Get it off me." As soon as the words left her mouth, his hands were sliding under her top, ripping it in two in one smooth motion. He tore the scraps from her body, tossing them carelessly to the side, her bra and jeans quickly joining the scrap pile. She looked up at him as his hand traced a trail of goosebumps from her stomach to her breasts.

He ducked his head, dark, red hair falling over his eyes as he took one of her nipples into his mouth, his tongue hot against her skin. His body temperature was rising with his arousal, steam leaving his mouth in soft wisps and moistening her flesh. She gripped his head with both hands as he sucked and rolled her nipple around with his tongue, pulling away to a blow hot, steamy breath across the hardened bud before taking the other into his mouth.

She cried out, feeling his cock rutting against her leg, seeking any kind of friction. "Please, please, please," she whispered. He pulled off her nipple, trailing scorching, open-mouthed kisses down her stomach to her thighs. She spread her legs instinctively, hands gripping his hair, guiding his searching mouth towards her clit. He muttered something in a deep, guttural tongue before he dove between her legs. He rolled the little bundle of nerves around with his tongue and she cried out softly, gripping his hair tight as she tossed her head back against the pillow. She could feel the heat creeping up her cheeks and just knew that her face must be bright red from the heat between her legs and the obscene noises Darius was making as he worked.

"Please," she begged again, and this time he relented, trailing sweltering kisses back up to her mouth. He licked between them, tongue rubbing against hers until she could taste herself, steam rising in swirling whirls between their mouths. She moaned against his lips and hooked her legs around his hips, tired of waiting. She could feel the fat head of his cock rubbing against her entrance and then he was pressing forward, slowly as she stretched to accommodate him. A whimper left her lips and he immediately stilled, cupping the side of her face.

"Are you all right?" He asked breathlessly, his expression strained as he fought to move his hips.

Alina inhaled, already nodding her head. "I'm okay. You can move."

He snapped his hips forward then, driving all the way to the hilt. She cried out but this time in pleasure, the feeling of being filled leaving her breathless and panting. Quickly finding their rhythm, they began to move together. The slow glide of him pulling almost all the way out and pushing back in was driving her crazy. Her arousal was building, but as soon as she was close, he would stop, denying her an orgasm. She could hear herself begging him again, faster, harder, faster, until his hips were snapping against hers with each thrust, shoving her further up the mattress until she had to put her hand out to stop herself from hitting the headboard. He took hold of her hips with his large hands, pulling her more firmly against him as her legs tightened around his hips, pulling him in deeper.

His steamy breath was fogging her room, the mirror above her dresser already clouded over with mist. Focusing on her mirror, her orgasm came out of nowhere, ripping through her body, as she called his name. She tightened around him while she climaxed, but he didn't slow his pace, fucking her through it. She knew he was closer when his rhythm stuttered, his thrusts growing sporadic and harder, ramming his hips against hers. He buried his face against her neck, breathing her name against the shell of her ear as he finished inside of her, and the sensation of his hot, scorching seed filling her was enough to make her come again.

She felt his ragged, hot breath across her throat, his heart thudding wildly in his chest above hers as she ran her fingers through his damp, sweaty hair. As soon as she caught her breath, she smoothed a strand of his hair back behind his ear. "We're going to need showers. *Again.*"

He raised his head from her neck, a hopeful smile on his lips. "Together?"

She laughed, leaning up to peck his lips. "Yes, we can take one together. But first, we need to go over some things about tomorrow." They laid in bed together, warmed by Darius's body heat and the streaks of pale sunlight that streamed through the open windows, their conversation drifted from planning their escape to their favorite foods and childhood memories while the sun slowly traveled across the sky.

She pressed her cold toes against his leg, hiding a smile against his shoulder. "I think I'm ready for that shower now." She said and squealed as Darius picked her up, carrying her over his shoulder easily into her adjoining bathroom. He set her down on the cool tile floor, pressing open mouth kisses against the long column of her neck.

She swatted at him playfully. "Wait for me to get the water going." She said and smothered a giggle behind her hand. She fiddled with the controls of the shower before finally deeming it the right temperature and held open the shower door for him. He stepped in slowly and she looked up at him as he brushed past her, eyes locking on his mouth. He dipped his head just as she stepped into the shower beside him, warm water sliding between them as their lips met in a soft kiss. He ran his fingers through her long hair, sweeping it over her shoulder and down her back all while keeping the kiss slow and gentle.

She could feel his cock against her thigh, long and heavy as it began to fill. His hands slid down her wet skin towards her ass, kneading the twin mounds of flesh as his tongue began to probe between her lips into her mouth. The wet slide of their tongues made her entire body shudder and soon the sound of her moans filled the small, enclosed space of the shower.

"I have no more patience for bathing," he said, and she squeaked as he gripped her under the thighs, lifting her up. She wrapped her arms around his neck as he walked them, dripping wet into her bedroom.

"Wait, wait!" She cried, trying to kick her legs and escape his hold. "You'll get my blankets all wet!"

He dropped her on the mattress, chuckling. "I think you'll forgive me." She shivered, the water from their warm shower quickly turning cool against her skin, turning her nipples into hardened pebbles. She looked up at him, watching his hand trace a trail of goosebumps from her stomach to her breast. He ducked his head, dark hair falling across his face as he took one of her nipples into his mouth, his tongue hot against her cool skin. She gripped his head with both hands as he sucked and rolled her nipple around with his tongue, pulling away to blow hot hair across the hardened bud before taking the other one into his mouth.

She cried out, feeling him rutting against her leg, seeking friction. "Please, please, please," she heard herself beg. "Now, please, I can't wait any longer." She confessed and felt his lips twist up around her nipple. She groaned, part in pleasure, part because she knew he was intent on torturing her now. He pulled off her nipple, trailing hot, open-mouthed kisses down her stomach to her thighs. She spread her legs, fingers gripping his hair, guiding his mouth towards her clit. He looked up at her, forest green eyes twinkling before he dove between her legs, tongue lathing against her clit. He rolled the little bundle of nerves around with his tongue and she cried out softly, gripping his hair tight as he drew it into his mouth and sucked. As she lay there with his head between her legs, his tongue licking eagerly inside her while his thumb circled her clit, she couldn't help but think that she could get used to this.

CHAPTER SIX

Alina walked with confidence down the boardwalk, her heels clicking a quick rhythm. Her arm was tucked into Darius's elbow as they made their way towards their awaiting ship. If there's one thing Alina knew, it was that if you looked like you should be there, no one would question whether you should be. They stopped in front of the plank leading to the ship where Alicia was waiting for them with her father. Alicia's father was a stern man with greying black hair and eyes the color of steel.

"Holy shit, Alina!" Alicia exclaimed, her eyes dragging over Darius. "Now, I see why you're so eager to, uh, jump ship as it were."

Alina groaned. "Please, no puns this early in the morning. I just can't handle it."

Alicia cackled. "I like your secret agent get up. I'm sure no one expected a thing what with you walking around New York dressed up like Black Widow." She said, motioning to Alina's tight black outfit.

"Shut up." Alina said, a blush rising on her cheeks. "I didn't want to draw attention to myself."

"No, yeah, a skintight little black number is exactly what I wear when I don't want to draw attention to myself." She said, bobbing her head in a nod.

"Ladies, ladies." Her father, otherwise known as Captain Vane, interrupted. "I have a schedule to keep and I believe we're supposed to avoid making a scene."

"Sorry, Daddy." Alicia said, her tone sickly sweet, making Alina roll her eyes. She pinched Alina's chin, her tone changing into one more serious. "Be careful, Lina. Let me know when you're safe."

Alina pulled her arm free of Darius to wrap her friend in a tight hug. "I will. I promise." She slowly let Alicia slip from her embrace, her smile watery.

Alicia nodded, wiping a few tears from the corner of her eye. "I just hope you won't regret this, Lina."

Alina threaded her fingers together with Darius. "I won't."

Darius nodded politely at Alicia and Captain Vane. "I promise that no harm will come to her. I give you both my word."

"Come on, I have a schedule to keep, remember?" Captain Vane said, ushering them both up the loading plank and onto the massive, magnificent ship. Alicia craned her head to get one last look at her friend before Captain Vane was guiding them below deck. "You both are very lucky.

On a cargo ship this large I usually have a crew of at least 50 men, but not for this voyage. We have plenty of extra space for you."

"How many men do you have on board?" She asked, struggling to navigate the narrow, steep stairs in her heels. She knew she shouldn't have worn these boots...Although they looked great with this outfit.

"Six." He answered truthfully, albeit hesitantly.

"Six?" She echoed, squeaking as the ship rumbled to life under her feet, making her stumble as it began to move out of the harbor. "Captain Vane... That doesn't seem right. Can only six men really-

"This is a routine delivery to Cork, Alina. Ireland really isn't that far from New York." He said, his tone making it clear that that was the end of the conversation.

Alina felt dizzy as she let the news wash over her, but it was too late. They were already moving out into the Atlantic in this massive steel cargo ship, crewed by six men. A sense of foreboding, a little worm of doubt, began to wriggle in her thoughts but she had to trust Captain Vane. She was best friends with his daughter and had known him for most of her life, she was sure he would never do anything to put her purposefully in danger.

"Here, this will be your room for the duration of the journey." He said, swinging a door open to their left. It was a simple room with a double bed, a dresser, and a lone work desk, the steel walls were painted a light cream colored.

Alina smiled quickly, trying to overcome the sudden surge of dread. "This will be fine, thank you, Captain Vane, for everything that you've done for us." She paused. "Um, how far down are we?"

"You're on deck three." He answered.

"How many decks are there?" She asked.

"Four." He said simply, turning on his heel to leave. "Now, if that's all, I can assure you that I'm needed elsewhere. Someone will be by to show you where you can take your meals."

"Oh, right, I'm sorry." She said but she was talking to his back as he made his way back to the main staircase. She tugged Darius by the arm into their room, closing the door and taking a deep, shuddering breath. She could feel her heart rate already calming, her worries soothed away by Darius's hands caressing her face and neck.

"Are you alright, my Lina?" He asked, his voice soft, just barely a whisper among the noises of the ship.

"Yeah, I just-" she stopped herself, tired of pretending that everything was fine when it wasn't.

"No, does this seem a little weird to you? I mean, this ship is *huge* and we're two of *nine* people on board."

"It does seem strange, yes. But you trust this man, don't you?" He asked.

"Yeah, Alicia has been my friend almost my entire life. I've known her father almost my whole life too." She said.

"Then I'm sure this Captain knows exactly what he's doing." He said and cupped her face in his hands. "But just in case, we will stay extra close."

She laughed softly. "Right, just for safety?"

"Just for safety." He repeated, taking her suitcase from her hands, and tossing it towards the dresser.

"Hey!" She protested. "If you knew how much that set cost you would not be throwing it around like that."

"Sh..." He murmured; his lips already pressed to the corner of her mouth. She turned her head, almost instinctively, her mouth searching for his. Their lips met in a gentle kiss, sending sparks racing down her spine, igniting in her belly. His large hand cupped the back of her head, keeping her in place as his tongue plundered her mouth. She moaned quietly at the first wet slide of his tongue against hers, her hands curling into fists, bunching up the soft fabric of his t-shirt between her fingers. A firm knock on the door had them springing apart, wiping their mouths with the backs of their hands, their cheeks flushed like teenagers caught with the door closed.

"Yeah, I'm knocking so someone can open the door because judging by the sounds coming from in there, I don't want to open it myself." A lilting, accented voice called out from the other side of the door.

Alina practically dove for the doorknob, yanking the door open. "We weren't-I mean, we just got here, we were just exploring." She said quickly.

"Yeah, just if you keep the exploring confined to that side of the door, love." The crew member said. He was a tall, slimly built young man. Alina pegged him somewhere in his early twenties. His bottle blonde hair was mussed in a way that was supposed to look natural but most likely involved a lot of product and his grey-blue eyes were staring intently into hers with poorly disguised interest. "Ah, now I see why the good Captain was so keen to make all those exceptions." He continued, dragging his eyes up her body.

"Ah," Darius said, his tone mocking as he stepped up beside her, sliding his arm around her waist. "And you must be the little sailor boy the good Captain sent to give us the tour." He said and next to Darius's hulking height and muscle, he did look much smaller.

"Alright, I get it, you two are a thing. Jesus, you can stop posturing now unless you'd like to piss a circle around her, mate." He said, rolling his eyes upward as if asking for strength. "I'm James, and just so you don't snap my neck later, I'm completely, utterly gay. So, unless your girlfriend has a-"

Alina cleared her throat, effectively cutting him off. "It's a pleasure to meet you, James, but like Darius was implying, we really would like to see the rest of the ship."

"Well, most of its off limits to non-crew but I'll show you as much as I can." He said. "Just stick close, this is a big ship and I don't want to have to go searching for you." He walked towards the main staircase, throwing a glance at them over his shoulder to make sure they were following. "You're the only ones on the third deck, and Captain Co-" He coughed suddenly. "I mean, Captain Vane, already gave the word he doesn't want you going any lower in the ship for whatever reason." He hopped up the staircases easily, leaving Darius to steady Alina who was wobbling in her heels. "This is deck two, has more bunks, and the cafeteria."

"Oh!" Alina interjected. "Can we grab a snack. I'm *starving*."

She caught a glimpse of James's eyes rolling upwards again before he was spinning around in the apparent direction of the cafeteria. "I guess, the longer I'm with you the longer I have until I have to go back down."

She smiled a little. "The voyage just started, James, you can't possibly be sick of your job already."

"I'm not sick of my job, I'm just a little concerned that we're crossing the Atlantic in an ancient hunk of steel with a crew of nine people. I'm still hoping it's a fucking dream actually, otherwise we are in very big trouble." James said.

As soon as the words left his lips, Alina felt her heart drop to her stomach. "James, what do you mean ancient?"

"Uh, I mean this ship is ancient, old, should be an actual museum. Or did you just not notice the smokestacks, love?" He said.

"Oh, I just-I thought they were decorative. You know, to make the cargo ship look...cooler." She said, mentally wincing as she spoke the words aloud and realized how stupid they sounded.

James cackled. "*Cargo* ship? Where the hell do you think you are? This is a passenger vessel, the only one left in Vane's fleet that hasn't been scrapped." He shrugged. "Like I said, I was hoping this was a dream because otherwise I'm actually part of a skeleton crew on an ancient passenger vessel, attempting to cross the Atlantic with two fugitives." He tsked, wagging his finger at them. "And before you flip, yes, obviously I know who the big guy is. He's pretty hard to miss in the papers."

"Oh my God..." Alina groaned. "This is a disaster."

"You're telling me, love." James said as he swung open the door to the cafeteria. "I'm pretty sure the only reason I'm here is so that Vane can drown me with fewer witnesses."

The corners of Darius's mouth quirked up in a small, amused smile. "Does the ...Good Captain, as you call him, dislike you?"

"Dislike me? He fucking hates me." He said, lifting one of his shoulders in shrug. "My buddy in HR says he keeps trying to figure out a way to fire me without running into a lawsuit. Unlucky for Vane that I'm actually amazing at my job." He said and slid over the cafeteria counter, digging through one of the cabinets before tossing a chocolate muffin towards Alina. Darius caught it in one hand before it could hit her in the face, spraying her hair with crumbs.

"Gee, thanks." She said flatly, accepting the remains of the muffin from Darius's cupped palms. She watched warily for any other flying bits of pastry as James hopped back over the counter, plopping at one of the tables.

He waved his hand around haphazardly. "Sit, eat. I already told you, don't feel like going back down yet. I said I thought Vane might like to drown me but the way he put me in the coal room makes me think he'd rather see me suffocate."

"What do you mean?" She asked.

He rolled his eyes. "God, you really are this clueless, aren't you? I mean only that we've been on fire since before we left the harbor, now he's trying to push us at top speed." He said, and her fingers tightened around the muffin, pulverizing what little was left intact.

"On *fire*?" She said, choking on a bit of chocolate she had inhaled in her shock. "Do you mean to tell me that the ship is on *fire*?"

"Oh...The Good Captain didn't tell you before you boarded?" He asked. "A fire started in the coal room last night while we were getting the ship ready. Don't wet your knickers, love, coal fires used to break out all the time in these old hunks of junk. It's not going to spread out of the coal room. Even the Titanic was on fire the entire time they were sailing." He said.

Alina's skin went startlingly pale as the blood drained from her face. "Yeah, could you maybe use any other comparison?"

Darius looked between them curiously. "I take it this ship, the Titanic, it did not reach port."

"No," Alina answered. "It didn't."

"But that's just because it hit an iceberg," James was quick to interject, "and trust me, we aren't hitting any of those. Not with this weather." He reached over, snagging a muffin chunk. "Although, if you don't see me when we reach Cork, tell them it was Vane."

"Can you not trust your comrades to watch your back?" Darius asked.

"Maybe if I had any here." James muttered bitterly.

"Aw, do you not have any friends? What a surprise." She said.

"Oh, fuck off, I have friends," he said, pelting her in the forehead with the muffin chunk. "The Good Captain just decided not to include any of them on our voyage. The five other guys here I've never actually met. Total muscle heads though, almost as big as your boy there." He said but Alina was hardly listening, she was focused on that little black hole of dread that was growing bigger in her mind.

"Wait, wait...You've never met the other members of the crew?" She asked.

James shook his head. "Nah, never seen any of them before. Which is a little odd, I guess, but it's a big shipping company. Why?"

Alina stood abruptly. "I have to talk to Captain Vane." She said.

James eyed her warily. "You're not allowed up on the deck, Cap's orders."

"If you know who we are then you know how *dangerous* we are. Take me to Captain Vane. Now." She said, grateful as Darius place a warm, supportive hand on her lower back.

"Alright, alright. No need to threaten so bloody much." He mumbled and swung his long legs out of the table. "Come on then, we're going this way." He said and led then out the door and up the grand staircase to the top of the deck. As they walked up into the fresh, salty air coming off the sea Alina was shocked to see how far they already were from the harbor. She could hardly see it anymore. *James wasn't joking when he said that they were moving at top speed.* She moved ahead of him, her heels clicking against the deck before she rapped her knuckles firmly against the door of the steering room.

"Captain Vane!" She shouted. "I need to speak with you, it's urgent." She startled back into Darius's firm chest as Vane yanked open the door, addressing James.

"What is she doing up here?" He demanded. "I

thought my instructions were clear."

"Yeah, you try to tell her and her beast where they aren't allowed be." He said.

"Captain Vane," she tried again. "Were you ever going to tell me that the ship is on fire? Why are we even on a ship this old? The whole point of this is to look inconspicuous and we look pretty conspicuous to me, Captain. There's something that you're not telling us."

"I'm not telling you that granting you this favor is putting me and my entire family at legal risk, not to mention my business, and the livelihoods of my men. Now, we're on this ship because it's the fastest one I have and I have specifically ignored safety violations so that you and your boyfriend will be less likely to run into anyone aboard with ship with a cellphone and penchant for reward money. Is that enough explanation for you or would you like me to continue?" He asked, staring her down.

"No," she said softly, guilt eating away at her. "No, I'm so sorry. We won't be any more trouble. I swear." She turned, allowing herself to melt into Darius's comforting embrace. "Let's go back to our room," she whispered. "I've had enough exploring."

Captain Vane called out to the three of them as they were retreating below, "James!" He called. "Remind me when we get to Cork, I'd like to have a little chat about your employment contract."

CHAPTER SEVEN

"Just perfect." James muttered as he stalked down the stairs. "Looks like he has a reason to fire me now."

"James," Alina said, pausing. "I'm *so* sorry. I didn't realize you might lose your job. Is there-"

"Look, love, I told you that you weren't supposed to be up there. You just didn't care; you can save the apologies for the next bloke you inevitably get fired." He said, hopping to the bottom of the stairs in one smooth motion. "I'll see you around probably. Try not to get crushed under that one." He said with a flippant wave towards Darius before disappearing to the second deck.

Alina sighed. "Well, I've completely ruined his day and Captain Vane hardly seems pleased with me. I guess we should just keep our heads down for the rest of the voyage."

Darius held open the door to their bunk. "I might have an idea how to pass the time." He said, his lips curling in a little smirk before his hands curled around her waist, tugging her off her feet.

She squeaked, instinctively wrapping her legs around his waist, her hands scrambling to grip his broad shoulders. "I don't think I will ever get over how strong you are." She said but he only laughed, effortlessly carrying her the rest of the way to their double bed. He carefully laid her out on the blankets and rose back up, chest falling and rising with his heavy breath as he stared down at her. The low light in their little cabin casted his skin in gold and in his eyes the embers of a low fire burned, making her hips shift almost of their own accord.

A slow smirk pulled over his face as he watched her squirm under his heated gaze. He fell forward over her, forcing her thighs to part for him. With his arms braced on either side of her head, he leaned down, keeping eye contact as he pressed their lips together in a hungry kiss. Their teeth clicked together before his lips moved down her neck and shoulder, the scrape of his scruff drawing breathless gasps from Alina's mouth. Darius pulled her up briefly to yank the skintight black top over her head, tossing it towards the floor. His fingers were rough as they fumbled with the buttons on her black skinny jeans.

She was quick to catch his hands in hers. "I packed light. I don't need you ripping these." She said and popped the button free, wriggling her hips as she tried to squirm out of the tight denim. Her bra and panties were quick to join the rest of her clothes on the floor and second later his lips were latched around the nub of a nipple. She tossed her head back against the pillow, a whine escaping her lips as she arched her breasts closer to his mouth. **He switched between both her breasts, suckling, and nipping at the hard nubs of her nipples.** He released her poor abused breast to kiss her briefly, his skin already beginning to heat under her touch.

He yanked his shirt over his head, his chest heaving as he stared down at her. "Alina…I know we haven't known each other long but from the moment I first laid eyes on you I was drawn to you. I love you." He said and leaned down to press a tender kiss against her lips.

She could feel her heart racing in her chest, but she wasn't afraid, she had been feeling the same deep connection between them. She broke free from his kiss. "Darius, I left *everything* to be with you. Of course, I love you." She said.

He smiled, lighting up his entire face before he dropped down to his knees off the bed, dragging Alina to the edge so her legs hung off into the chilly cabin air. He made a little sound in the back of his throat, gently prying her knees farther apart. Alina's fingers twisted in the bedding beside her, already anticipating the feeling of his mouth on her but Darius did nothing for what felt like an eternity before she felt his lips on the underside of her knee.

He worked his way up her milky thigh with a methodical slowness, pressing featherlight, open-mouthed kisses all over her inner thighs. When he reached the crease of her thigh he paused, laughing a little against her leg, his hot breath gusting across sensitive skin. The sensation pulled a whimper from her throat, her sex throbbing with need. Darius's laugh quickly turned into a groan, sliding a rough cheek against her sensitive inner thigh before moving to kiss her other knee. He repeated the same agonizing process along that leg. She thumped him in the back of her head with the heel of her foot, thanking every deity she could think of for granting her flexibility.

"Darius..." She whined as he hovered there again, the steamy caress of his breath making her throb with need. Darius gave another little chuckle before he braced his arms and went back to work, pressing his tongue flat and giving her one long, slow lick. He flicked his tongue around the little nub of her clit, stroking more firmly with his tongue as he dipped inside her folds. Her head writhed back and forth against the blankets, the sounds of her desire slipping from her parted lips as she experienced a pleasure so intense, she felt as if she might burst apart at the seams. Darius continued the strong, firm strokes with his tongue through her orgasm, wringing every bit of sinful pleasure from her before pulling back, a wicked look in his eyes as his tongue traced his lips.

"I can't feel my legs. I think you crippled me." She said, her voice wobbling.

"I'll take that as a compliment." He chuckled, crawling back up her body, tugging her up the mattress with him. She watched, already thoroughly sated as he tugged off his own jeans, his long. thick cock jutting out from the apex of his muscled thighs. Darius watched her for a few moments, his breath leaving little clouds of steam, his fingers in constant motion as he traced her collarbone, her cheek, and the line of her jaw. He stared at her, his eyes tracing the shape of her face and when he finally spoke, his voice was barely a whisper. "I only wish for you to be happy. I hope that I'm able to provide that for you."

Words struggled to come; how could you tell someone how much they meant to you when you could barely find the words to make sense of it yourself? Luckily, Darius dipped his head and kissed her again, silencing any response she had. He worked himself between her milky thighs once more, his body still impossibly large over hers. She squeezed her thighs against his as he braced himself with one muscular arm, the other trailing down between their bodies. He pressed a tender kiss to the base of her throat as he gently skimmed her folds with the pads of his fingers, drawing a small gasp from her lips. He licked a firm stripe up her neck, his breath hot and moist against her throat as he sank a finger into her, his other hand caressing her cheek gently.

Darius worked his finger in and out slowly, the roughness of his hands drawing gasps and moans from her as she tried to rock her hips back against his hand. He kept the pace slow and gentle, slipping in a second finger the next time he pushed in and Alina moaned, her hands knotting themselves into his mussed hair. "Please," she begged, her hips thrusting to meet each push of his fingers.

She let out a disappointed sound as his fingers slipped free from between her folds. Darius grabbed one of her legs, hooking it in the crook of his arm before pushing it up high as his cock nudged her entrance. She wasn't sure she'd ever get used to the feeling of his rigid cock filling her so deep, forcing her to stretch around its girth. Her breath came in shallow pants as she tried to accommodate him, nodding when she noticed he was waiting to continue. Darius grunted when his hips finally met the back of her thighs, stilling above her again, their foreheads pressed together as their steamy breath mingled.

Darius pinched her chin between his thumb and index finger, tipping her head down for a kiss as he pulled his hips back and then rolled them forward in a smooth, shallow thrust. Alina moaned loudly, tossing her head back against the pillows as she gripped at his shoulders. Darius continued his smooth, shallow thrusts, driving deeper with each roll of his hips until Alina was writhing in pleasure, sure that his arms were the only thing keeping her from coming apart underneath him. He moved suddenly, sitting back on his knees, and, with his hands gripping her hips tightly, lifted her up until she was completely sheathed on his cock.

Her fingers dug into the bulky meat of his shoulders, her head tilted back, mouth open. "Ah! Darius!" She called. His thumbs stroked quick circles on her hips before snapping his hips up, setting a fast rhythm of short, forceful thrusts. He fixed his grip on her, bouncing her in his lap to meet each powerful thrust of his hips. Their room filled quickly with the noise of her shouts and the wet slap of skin on skin. Her shouts grew in volume as he found that spot inside her that made sparks shoot up her spine all the way to her fingertips. His answering smirk was all the warning she got before he changed his angle, hitting that spot with each snap of his hips. Her eyes slammed shut, stars bursting against the darkness as she screamed and came for the second time that night.

Darius fell back, planting his feet on the bed and thrust up against her with a newfound force, grunting with each plunge of his cock. Alina moaned softly, trying to keep balance as the friction sent her nerves into overdrive. Darius slammed his hips upwards once more, steam pouring from his nostrils as he came, filling her with his seed. When he was finished, she finally toppled over onto his chest, sighing happily as she felt his fingers combing through her hair. "I did not hurt you, did I?" He asked her gently and she could detect the hint of worry in his tone.

She lifted her head, catching his lips in a soft, pure kiss. "I love you." She said against his mouth and felt his answering smile. Darius reached out, somehow freeing the blanket, and tugged it over them. He ran a finger down her cheek before curling his arms around her waist. He kissed the top of her hair, smiling as his eyes slipped shut. "I love you, Alina, more than I can possibly explain."

***

A hard knock on the door awoke them hours later from the cocoon of blankets they found themselves in. Alina groaned softly, rolling gracelessly out of bed. Her knees buckled, and she sent a dirty look towards Darius who was watching her through half-lidded eyes. "I'm *sore*." She grumbled, hastily trying to wriggle back into her clothes which were strewn all around the floor.

"I would apologize but you really didn't sound like you had any complaints at the time." He said, a smug smirk on his lips.

"I'll remember that you said that." She warned before pulling open their cabin door.

"Oh my God." James said instantly, his eyes widening as he stared at something above her eyes."

"What?!" She squeaked, ducking, and looking over her in a panic.

James cackled. "What did you do to your *hair*?" He asked, and she could see the exact moment realization dawned in his eyes. "Oh, gross. Never mind. I do not want to know. Your shirt is on backwards by the way. Might want to fix that before we go to dinner, which is now." He said and peered past her into their room. "You too, big guy. Foods only going to be warm for so long."

"It's kind of you to come and get us, especially

after how we parted." Darius said as he climbed out of bed, still completely nude.

"Yep, okay. I'm never forgetting that image. Thanks for that, mate." He said, turning back to Alina with a mock whisper. "You had that thing in you? It's as thick as my wrist, *limp*!"

"It is not-" She stopped herself, huffing softly as she adjusted her shirt and combed her fingers through her, admittedly, wild hair. "It just takes... practice." She finally said, glancing over her shoulder to find Darius back in his clothes, looking as pristine as he had before their afternoon activities. "Really? Is that just something in your genetics? You just look perfect all the time?" She asked.

"I do not understand...Are you displeased with my appearance?" He asked, his head tilting slightly.

"Never mind." She sighed, looking hopefully at James. "Food? I'm starving."

"Yeah, I bet you are." He said, leading them back up the stairs and to the cafeteria. Once again it was eerily empty, the faint smell of bread and baked chicken hugging the air.

"I don't see anyone here. Where are the cooks?" She asked.

"Captain Vane didn't sign any on for this trip." James replied. "One of the new guys came up about an hour ago and made some chicken soup and rolls. It's still hot."

"That sounds perfect, thanks." She said, and James just stared at her.

"Well go and get it yourself, I'm not your waiter, love." He said. "Wait, I'll get it. I don't want to hear what you get up behind the counters." He winked as he hopped up and slid over the counter back into the kitchen.

Alina lowered herself to the table with a sigh, sharing an exasperated look with Darius. "I'm not the only one of us that finds him really tiring, right?"

"No, his presence is indeed exhausting."

"I heard that, and I spit in your soup." James said, plopping two steaming bowls in front of them. "Just kidding. Eat up." He straddled the bench seat, feigning disinterest as he picked at his nails. "So, what they're saying on the news...Can you really turn into a fucking dragon? Because, I have to tell you, that would be both awesome and disastrous to see right now."

Darius smiled indulgently. "Yes, I am from an ancient line of dragon shifters. Alina has dragon blood in her veins as well. Though, I doubt it is enough to allow her a complete transformation."

Alina sipped at her soup, allowing her mind to drift as the two men began to talk eagerly about flight and whether Darius could breathe fire. She worried her bottom lip between her teeth, her feeling of unease on this ship only seemed to grow the more time they spent on it. She was eating slowly; Darius and James still hadn't broken their conversation to eat when she began to feel it. It was like slow moving webs wrapping around her mind, all coherent thoughts slipping through the webbing. Her movements became more sluggish and she struggled to grasp onto any concrete ideas. One errant thought stuck suddenly, and she stopped, her spoon halfway to her lips. "James... If this was a passenger vessel then where to they keep all the steel your transporting?" She asked slowly.

He finally looked at her, his eyebrows shooting towards his hairline. "Shit, you all right, love? You look like you're going to fall into your soup."

"Answer...Answer my question." She struggled to say and felt Darius wrap and arm around her waist to steady her.

"You're not making any sense. We're not transporting any steel unless you count monster of a kennel down near the hull."

She could almost feel her heart stutter to a stop, the sudden adrenaline rush sharpening her dulled senses. "It's a trap. The men Vane hired; they must have set a trap." She said quickly, struggling to rise from the table.

Darius helped her up, his face all sharp angles and tension. He brought his bowl of soup to his lips, taking a cautious sip only to spit it to the side with a snarl. "This is poisoned." He turned towards James, fury glowing like deep red embers in his eyes. "You did this!"

He held up his hands. "I had no idea! I swear, mate." Darius reached down, yanking James's bowl close to his face, soup sloshing over the sides as his nostrils flared to scent it.

"Yours is poisoned too." He finally said, hurling the bowl across the room with a clatter of noise and soup.

"Those fucking pigs!" James said, jumping to his feet. "We need to get off this boat. If we take a lifeboat now, nightfall will cover our escape. They won't come looking for our bodies until they're sure the poison did its job. We need to go now."

"No." Darius disagreed, his posture stiff and his chest heaving as he tried to control his rage. "If we run now they will only follow. We have to finish this here." He caught Alina as she tipped to the side. "I will go take care of your fellow crewmen. Take Alina to the lifeboats, get one prepared. I will meet you on deck."

James nodded, wrapping his arm around Alina's waist, hauling her to her feet. "If you're not back by the time the suns all the way down, well, let's just say I'm not planning on dying today."

Darius clasped his shoulder, squeezing it tightly, ignoring his hiss of pain. "I understand. Just keep her safe." He released his shoulder to lay a gentle hand on her cheek. "I will return to you when this is over. I swear it."

She lifted a shaking hand, covering his. "Be careful."

James and Alina shuffled towards the exit of the cafeteria. He stopped for a moment, calling back over his shoulder. "Oi! Dragon boy, try not to set fire to the ship until after we're off it, yeah?" Darius's low rumbling laugh followed them out.

CHAPTER EIGHT

"You know, you're a lot heavier than you look, love." James muttered breathlessly as he hauled her up step after step. "It'd be really great if you could sober up right about now." He spat out a piece of her hair that got caught in his mouth as her head lolled onto to his shoulder. "That a no then? Right, no, this is fine." He said with a grunt of effort. "We're almost there anyway so it's not like I'd love the help."

She groaned. "Do you *ever* shut up?"

"Only when I got my mouth full." He said, smirking down at her.

"Yeah, you can stop there. I don't need the mental image." She said.

"Well, I sure as bloody hell didn't need the picture I got when I came to collect you for dinner but that didn't seem to matter to you." He stopped briefly on the stairs to catch his breath.

"Maybe if you didn't talk so much you wouldn't be so out of breath." She suggested, her energy slowly starting to return to her.

"And maybe if you didn't have such a gigantic arse weighing you down we'd be at the top by now."

"As soon as you have the lifeboat ready, I'm pushing you overboard." She said, and James laughed breathlessly, helping her up the last flight of stairs. They both took a huge breath of the cool, ocean air as soon as they pushed the doors open. The sun was only halfway down the horizon, painting the ocean in liquid gold. She couldn't help the gasp that escaped her. "The sunset...it's so beautiful on the water."

"Yep, don't really have time for that so let's-" James was interrupted by a thundering roar echoing beneath their feet before they were suddenly thrown to the side as the ship tipped to the right. They tumbled to the deck, sliding towards the railings. Alina's hands and feet scrambled on the slick surface of deck, trying to find anything to grab to keep her from being flung overboard. James caught her hand, his other was white knuckled on the leg of a sundeck bench that had been bolted to the deck. "Hold on! She'll right herself, give her a moment." The ship rocked back to the left, sending them sliding back the other way.

Alina groaned as the ship finally settled enough for them to stand. "I'm going to have strong words with him about that."

James rolled his shoulders, rubbing his arms. "Speak for yourself. Can you walk on your own now?" He said, sighing when she nodded. "Good. Follow me, we have to lower the boat into the water." He walked quickly to the other side of the deck where the lifeboats were strung up.

"If we lower it now then how will we get in?" She asked. "Won't it just float away? Have you even done this before?"

"Look, genius, we can't lower it while we're inside it. We'll have to climb down and it's not just going to float away. It will be anchored to the ship, we'll just have to cut the ties when we climb down." He said and grabbed onto a thick piece of rope hanging beside one of the boats. "We really don't have time for this. Just trust me and pull when I tell you to. I can't do this on my own."

She nodded, grabbing hold of the rope. "Okay." All the breath she had in her lungs left in one giant whoosh of air as a hand grabbed her hair, dragging her down. She landed hard on her back on the deck, her chest aching as she tried to draw air in. Captain Vane walked silently around her, a large wooden oar clutched in his hands. She finally got enough breath to shout "James!" And watched as he turned back to look at her just in time for the paddle of the oar to crack across his face. He dropped to the deck, unmoving.

"I always hated that little fag." Captain Vane said offhandedly.

"Oh God, James..." She choked as she tried to crawl towards his body, crying out as Vane reached down, fisting his hand in her hair.

"Nu uh, you're coming with me, missy." He said, dragging her by the hair towards the Captain's cabin. "You've been a naughty girl." She scrambled to get her feet under her to relieve some of the pressure on her scalp, her fingers clawing at his wrist.

"Let me go!" She shrieked as he kicked open the door to his cabin.

"That *hurts* you little bitch!" He shouted and threw her roughly against his dresser. She hit the corner of the wooden dresser hard, wheezing as her ribs flared with a stabbing pain. She took a few short breaths before standing steady on her feet, turning to face him. She couldn't fight the tears that slipped down her cheeks as she stared into the eyes of the man she looked up to since she was a child.

"Why?" She finally choked out. "Your daughter is my best friend. I-I've known you almost my entire life." She said, flinching back closer to the dresser as he strode confidently towards her, quickly crossing the space between them.

"Oh, poor little Alina." He cooed, wiping at the tears on her cheeks. "Do you really think that I could stand you? You were always an entitled little brat, shaking your ass around my house." His thumb swept over her bottom lip. "Do you know what I'm going to do to you?" She shook her head and he smiled, leaning in to whisper against her ear. "Well, first I'm going to fuck you and then I'm going to chain you up in here with that little fag so you'll have someone to die with when the ship goes down. Then, I'm going to take that ridiculous man you've been whoring yourself to and I'm going to sell him back the labs for a massive profit. Don't worry about Alicia." He smirked. "She'll mourn you, but she'll have her father to help her through it."

"You're a monster..." She said, her body going numb as his horrifying words washed over her.

He laughed boisterously. "No, the monster is downstairs." His hand slithered up her side toward her breast, pushing her into motion. She brought her head forward, headbutting him in the nose. Pain exploded in her forehead but all she truly felt was satisfaction as his nose crunched, breaking under the force of her hit. She lunged to the side as he stumbled back with a cry, running for the door. A pained yelp left her lips as he caught her by the hair, throwing her against the side on his bed. He was on top of her before she could move, his weight sending searing pain through her damaged ribs.

He grabbed her roughly, turning her around to face him. "I want to see your tits while I fuck you." He growled, using his body weight to pin her against the side of the bed. He knocked her legs apart easily, settling heavily between her thighs. One hand gripped her hands over her head, the other squeezing tightly around her throat. She fought for each small, wheezing breath, her eyes watering, as the room began to go dark around her. She let her eyes slip close, the world slowing down to each strong thump of her heart. Each thud of her heart was magnified, her fingers tingling, as a long sleeping power crackled to life under her skin. She felt a rush of warmth surge from her chest all the way out to her fingers and toes, electrifying all her nerves.

Her eyes snapped open, glowing a deep ruby inside her skull. Vane released her throat and wrists with a shout, stumbling away from her as he observed his burnt hands, the blisters already forming over his palms. "What the hell did you do?!" He screamed but she ignored him, staring down at her open palm instead. Her veins pulsed the same ruby color as her eyes. She gulped giant breathes of air, steaming flying from her nose as she exhaled.

"That's interesting…" She muttered, drunk from the power she felt thrumming through her. She stepped towards in, her feet leaving scorch marks in the floor behind her.

"You bitch!" Vane cried, swinging his fist towards her. She caught the blow against the palm of her hand, digging her fingers into the top of his hand to stop his retreat as her flesh burnt his, making it crackle and pop under the blistering heat. He yanked away, cradling his mangled, burnt hand against his chest. He backed away from her, spitting, "witch," towards her as he retreated until his back was to the door. "Tell me, does that little trick protect you from bullets?" He pulled a pistol from the back of his pants, holding it steady towards the center of her chest.

She stopped abruptly, holding her hands up.

"Captain, let's just slow down, okay? No one needs to die. We can still all walk away from this."

"The only one that's going to walk away from this is me!" He shouted. Alina's eyes drifted to the side as a flash of movement caught her attention. Vane tried to follow her gaze, turning his head just in time to get caught in the face by the paddle end of an oar. He dropped to the floor, the gun skittering just out of reach. He groaned, blindly reaching towards it as blood poured renewed from his nose and now a cut above his eye.

"Nope. You go for that gun and the next time I hit you with this is going to be right in the cock." James said. Alina felt a surge of relief at seeing her new friend still alive. A trickle of blood ran from his nose and there was an impressive bruise already blossoming on the right side of his face but otherwise he looked unharmed. "Lina, love, you wanna grab that gun?" She quickly grabbed the gun, holding it awkwardly in her hands. "And then just pop the safety on? It's just on the side there, there you go, perfect. Not gonna comment on those eyes now, can't decide if they're pretty or just fucking scary." He said and looked down at Captain Vane. "What are we going to do with him?"

Alina's eyes didn't leave Vane's prone form, curled slightly on the ground. "He was...He was going to-"

"No, I get the gist. You don't have to go on, love." He said and stared back down at Vane. "You really are a slimy bastard, aren't you? Forget what I said. I'm hitting you in the cock anyway." He said and that was all the warning Vane got before he brought the oar down on his crotch. Maybe it would make Alina a bad person if she savored the man's screams...but she savored his screams. She watched the man she used to think of as a father and let the rage consume her once more. Her leg flew forward, her foot catching him in the face as she kicked him over and over again until James was grabbing her by the shoulders, trying to pull her back.

"Stop! Lina, stop! He's unconscious." James said, jerking his hands off her shoulders. "Fuck, that hurts. And your clothes are smoking by the way. So...if there's an off button, you might want to press it now."

Alina backed rapidly away from him, staring at her palms and the steam rising from her skin. "I-I don't know how."

"Right... we'll figure that out later then. In the meantime, it looks like your boy ripped a hole through the hull somehow. The ship is going down, we have to get off, now." He said and waved his hand at her to get her out the door. She nodded shakily and fled from the cabin, deliberately not looking at Captain Vane's body as she went. James shut the door to the cabin behind them. "I doubt he'll wake up. Besides, Captain goes down with the ship." They walked quickly back to the lifeboats, Alina's feet leaving a trail of blackened, charred footprints behind them. She reached automatically for the rope they had been trying to pull earlier, her mind slowly going numb as the day's events finally seemed to catch up with her.

"Alina, no!" James shouted, too late as her fingers curled around the rope. Flames erupted from the points her fingers touched, traveling up the rope and to the boats that were attached. She let it fall from her fingers, her eyes widening in horror at what she had done.

"No, no, no…" She muttered. "James, I'm-I'm so sorry. I wasn't thinking."

"There's nothing we can do about it now." He said quietly, his face resigned. They stood together, several feet apart because of the waves of heat emanating from Alina's body, and watched as the flames consumed their only means of escape while the ocean kept creeping steadily higher towards them. That was where Darius found them, still watching the inferno, as he ran towards them, naked and grinning from his success on the battlefield.

"They had a few tricks up their sleeves but no trickery is a match for my battle prowess." He boasted with a smile, his chest puffing up a little. "Why is everything on fire?" He asked finally.

"Thank your girlfriend for that, mate. Can you do something about that heat coming off her? I really don't want to be the only one here wearing clothes…" James answered.

Darius approached Alina eagerly, hesitating as

he regarded her solemn eyes staring into the fire. "Alina," he said gently. "You are injured...is that what triggered the awakening of your abilities?" He asked only to be met with silence.

"Yeah...She's had a bit of a rough night. Think you could just...turn them off or something?" James asked.

Darius gently cupped her cheek, the intense heat having no effect on him. He gripped her face a little more firmly when she almost flinched away from his caress. "Alina, it's me. Whatever happened to you on this night, it's over and I swear to you that I will always keep you safe. I won't leave you alone again." He vowed, ignoring James's muttered: "alone? Then what the hell was I?"

"Darius," she whispered, recognition finally sparking in her eyes before they gleamed with desperation. "Darius, you have to help me. Please, I can't control it." She begged, tears welling in her eyes.

"Sh..." He whispered. "I'm here. I'll take care of you now." He cupped the other side of her face, closing his eyes in concentration. "Sleep." He said firmly, and Alina fell forward against his chest as the power left her all at once, leaving her chilled and drained. He wrapped his arms around her, holding her up. "There, I have suppressed her abilities for now. Where is our escape boat that you mentioned earlier? I'm afraid I may have caused some serious damage below."

"Right there." James said, motioning to the

growing tower of flames. "Like I said, you can thank your girlfriend for that. Now we're stuck on a ship that's sinking *and* on fire which someone's going to see and come to arrest us."

A small smirk tugged at the corner of his mouth. "I wouldn't exactly say we are stuck." He helped Alina over to him. "Here, support her. I'll be back in a moment." He said before jogging towards the railing of the ship.

"Darius, what are you doing?" Alina called at the same time James said: "we really need to find him some clothes."

Darius climbed over the railing, turning around so that he could face them. His eyes twinkled mischievously, and he gave a jaunty wave before falling back towards the ocean.

"Darius!" Alina shrieked and shoved James's arm away as she ran to the railing, peering over it. She had to jump back as Darius swooped straight up towards her, his wings stretched out to catch the ocean winds and his scales gleaming brilliantly in the starlight. He shot overhead, twirling in the sky over the ship before landing on the deck with enough force to send it rocking from side to side in the water.

James took one step back, then another, eyeing the massive beast. "I...I am actually speechless." Alina grabbed him by the elbow, pulling him towards Darius who had lowered himself to his belly as he patiently waited for them.

"Come on, he's going to fly us off the ship." She

said, climbing up the rough, dark red scales on Darius's side to settle on his back.

"Where is he flying us to?" James asked, pulling himself up.

"Ireland!" Alina called to him; the noise of the wind being pushed by his enormous wings made it difficult to hear. "That's where we were headed before all this anyway. We'll regroup there." She held on the best she could as Darius suddenly launched them into the air, flying them up towards the stars before he leveled out, massive wings spreading to catch the wind as he glided them into the night.

End

THE DRAGON'S WAR

By Evelyn Winters

> "One day, you will be old enough to start reading fairytales again."
> ~C.S. Lewis, <u>The Chronicles of Narnia</u>

CHAPTER ONE

The stars were ablaze in the sky just beyond the heavy mist that settled over the Atlantic. Darius was flying low, hugging the churning waters to remain unseen from the search parties they could hear flying towards their wrecked former vessel. The result was cold and wet. The mist logged them down with a layer of sodden clothing that chilled in the icy North wind, the rolling sea below them occasionally mustering up a wave big enough to spray them over Darius's warm back. Both Alina and James were huddled down against his rough scales, pressed together for warmth.

Alina's wet hair was whipping in the wind, which felt like it was picking up, churning the sea until it looked like it was boiling beneath them. James's artfully tousled, bottle blond hair was plastered against his face. If she weren't so cold and miserable herself, she might have laughed, he was looking more and more like a wet, irritated cat. The night seemed to stretch on forever until the first golden rays of dawn began to pierce through their misty cover.

She didn't have to worry long about anyone

seeing a dragon soaring over the water, for just as the mist broke, they came upon rocky, red sanded beach enclosed by a circular formation of smooth, grey cliff face. Years of water battering against the walls left an opening, like the mouth of a large cave. Darius didn't need to hear them yelling over the wind to glide seamlessly inside. The cave of sorts was wide but not overly deep or tall, but it was a good enough hiding spot for now.

"Jesus, I am never doing that again." James's entire body was shaking, teeth chattering, and breaking the stillness of their hideout. "Did your boyfriend have to go so fucking slow? Or be that close to the water?"

"We could have left you on that boat to drown, you know, you should be thanking Darius, not making your bitchy comments." She snapped.

"Bitchy comments? Hm, let's see, why am I in this situation to begin with? Oh I don't know, maybe because I helped save you from Mr. Rapey and then you and your boyfriend decide to burn the ship down, oh yeah, and sink it. At the same time. Nice teamwork there, babe. Oh, and let's not forget who got me fired!" He pointed his trembling finger towards her, paused, then lowered it. "Wait, was I technically fired? Because Captain Vane was going to fire me as soon as we got on shore and we're on shore...But you killed Captain Vane-Oh, I'm sorry, left him for dead." He added when he saw the outrage on her face. "Because that's soooo much better." He muttered.

"Would you just shut up? God, I wish we back over the water, at least you were quiet." She said.

"Maybe I didn't want your boyfriend to break his concentration, ever think that I was being considerate?" He asked.

"No, you're never considerate." She stated, sniffling.

"You've known me for three days! I could be a goddamn saint for all-hey, where did your oaf, I mean, your boyfriend go?" He asked, scraping the wet hair back from his eyes as he looked around.

"Oh no, Darius..." Alina spotted him first, kneeling in the exact place that they had landed, his entire body trembling, though not from the cold. She ran to him, placing a comforting hand on his shoulder. "I'm so sorry. I should have checked on you right away, James baited me into an argument."

"I did no such thing!"

"Shut up!" She huffed, taking a deep, calming breath. "I'm sorry, are you hurt? I didn't even think-you must not be used to carrying people." She rubbed her hand over the knotted muscles in his back. "Are you all right?"

His smile was strained. "I'm perfectly all right, my Lina. It has been some time since I have flown that far, that is all. Being in captivity for so long didn't afford me many opportunities to stretch my wings." He caught her wrist, lifting it to his mouth. He pressed a kiss to her pulse point. "I will recover."

"I need to thank you. You saved our lives, Darius." She said, stroking the tips of her fingers down his stubble-rough cheeks.

James popped his hand in the air. "I'm not going to thank you, mate, I should be doing the opposite of thanking you-what is the opposite of thanking you? Well, when I figure it out, I'm going to do it. I shouldn't even *be* here right now. The two of you think you're so cute with your staring and your slow-mo cheek stroking, but you're destructive. That's the truth, you swept in and ruined my life and now we're going to starve in this shitty cave. That's if we don't drown first when the tide comes back in because am I the only one that can see that water line? Oh! My iPod!" His fist shot into the air triumphantly, iPod curled under his fingers. "It was in my pocket the whole time! I thought I left it on the ship, but it was in my pocket." He stuffed the left bud in his ear, grinning. "Hey! It still works." He started to bob his head, his lips puckering until he was making what was probably the most obnoxious duck face Alina had ever seen.

"Jesus Christ, you're retarded." Alina finally said.

"Hey… You can't use that word anymore, it's offensive." He said and started to whistle the chorus of Pumped Up Kicks.

"No, James, it isn't. In fact, I'd go as far as to say that the *only* time anybody can use that word is when they're trying to describe you. And Pumped Up Kicks, really? Do you even know what that song is about?" She asked incredulously.

"Yep." He popped the P, raising his middle finger to flip her off. "And I don't care. It's groovy."

"Groovy? I can't believe you actually just used that word."

"Enough." Darius said before James could retaliate. "Enough bickering." He staggered to his feet, taking a moment for his legs to stop shaking, and walked purposefully towards James. He stood in front of him, plucking the bud from his ear. "I understand why you are acting like this, James, you're upset."

"And you're standing really close for someone with their cock still out, mate."

Darius carried on. "You risked your life when you went back to help Lina and that's something I vow to repay you for someday." He clasped James's hand in a firm shake. "It was never my intention to put anyone in danger, especially someone who has proven to be a friend. I apologize."

Alina watched James stare back with eyes that were bugging with panic and lips that flapped open and then back closed, his hand still intertwined with Darius's. *Oh God,* she thought, *it looks like he's broken him.*

"Careful," the voice that came from the mouth of the cave was thick with an Irish brogue. "He self-combusts if you try to have a serious conversation with him."

Alina felt Darius's hand closing around her wrist, yanking her behind him. He stood in front of them both, green eyes glowing out of the darkness, steam pouring from his nostrils with each irritated huff at the intruder. "Leave now and I'll let you leave with your life."

James wiggled out from under one of Darius's muscled arms. "Yeah, please don't incinerate my boyfriend." His eyes were bright and his grin blinding. "Get down here you dramatic fuck. Stop trying to be creepy and mysterious."

The man that walked down into their cave was a head shorter than James and about as twice as stocky, thick cords of muscle pulling taut the dark navy trench coat he had on over his shoulders. He had dark brown, curly hair that flopped down to cover one startlingly bright blue eye in the damp and humidity of the cave. His mouth was set in a firm line, eyes still locked on Darius despite James practically vibrating for want of attention.

"Kieran!" James cheered and flung himself forward at the other man. He bent his knees so he could hang off his shoulders, staring up at him adoringly with the change in height. Kieran caught him by the slim waist despite making no move to take his eyes away from her boyfriend. James's grin was slowly falling. "Look, I know he has his cock out but I'm starting to get jealous here, babe, besides he's straight *and* taken *and* totes boring. Really you have no-" Kieran covered James's mouth and Alina savored the silence despite the tense atmosphere.

"You don't have permission to be here." Kieran

said and Darius seemed to relax at this statement, the tense set of his shoulders dropping.

"Ah, I thought your kind were all extinct." Darius said, taking her hand and squeezing it reassuringly.

"Almost." Kieran answered and James made a soft, confused noise behind his palm.

"Yes, they must be in trouble if they have a welp like you guarding their borders." Darius said.

"Darius!" She scolded. "You can't just call someone a...welp. Especially not after they got James to shut up."

"Ah, yes, my apologies. I suppose you wouldn't believe me if I said that we were just passing through?" Darius asked.

"I have to take you before the Tiarna, all of you." He seemed to at least regret the last part of this. "You couldn't have shown up at a worse time. Especially with *her*."

She frowned, "I'm sorry, do I know you?"

"No, but I know of you. We all do." He said and finally took his hand off James's mouth.

"Okay, can someone just tell me what the fuck is going on? I'm wet and freezing and someone tried to kill me a few hours ago and I'm not in the mood for riddles or for you arseholes to talk circles around each other." James said all at once, still hanging off Kieran's shoulders but now looking a little less adoringly at him.

"Your boyfriend is a fairy." Darius said as if that explained everything.

"Well that's just rude."

"No, darlin', he's not trying to be funny. If you saw what he is then it shouldn't be much of a shock, but I am what he says. I'm one of the Fae." He told him.

"So...it's not just this weird dragon bloke, is it? Shifters, Fae, how much of it is real?" James asked.

"How much of what?"

"The fairytales, you dick, how much of the fairytales are real? Is everything real? Are there other types of shifters? Are banshees real? Are kelpies and unicorns and Edward and Jacob?" He asked frantically, his voice raising a few octaves with each question asked.

"Darius?" Alina questioned. She had never thought about there being more than just the dragons.

"Most of it, not all." Kieran answered. "Not unicorns or vampires, though there are things like them. Werewolves are real, I guess, but not like those stupid movies you watch, they're shifters like him," he jerked his head towards Darius. "They just turn into wolves instead."

"Were you ever going to tell me?" He asked and for the first time since Alina met him, he wasn't buried under ten layers of bad humor and false confidence. He sounded younger. He sounded lost.

"I couldn't, darlin', there's laws I have to abide by." He said over the roar of the ocean. He glanced over his shoulder at the incoming tide. "The water's rising. You need to come with me if you want to pass through Ireland safely."

"Is that a threat?" Alina asked. "We're not going to stay longer than it takes to find another boat out of here."

Darius raised his hand towards her. "Peace, Alina. My kind were once allies to the Fae, we will speak with their king. He may even be able to lend us his aid." He walked forward, still naked, dragging Alina behind him. He grinned broadly, dipping his head in a nod towards Kieran. "Lead on."

***

"This is absolutely fucking ridiculous. I'd just like to have that on record." James stated, arms crossed over his slight chest. Alina was grinning from the passenger seat of the Land Rover, unable to help herself.

"Surely twenty minutes in my lap won't wound your manly pride." She said.

"Darlin', if you don't get in this car in the next thirty seconds, I'm leavin' you here." Kieran added stoically from the driver's seat. James narrowed his eyes at his boyfriend but seemed to take the threat seriously. He groaned, making an overexaggerated show of folding himself into the land rover, plopping harder than necessary down on her lap.

Alina choked. "How does someone who looks so skinny weigh so much?"

"Hey, this wasn't exactly my idea, love. Tell me again what I did to deserve your company?" He asked, sarcasm dripping out of his mouth.

"Because Darius didn't want me in your lap and Kieran didn't want you in Darius's. It's twenty minutes, I think you'll live." She answered and waited if he would point out that she could have sat in Darius's lap. It's not that she didn't want to, she just didn't want to be so close to Kieran. There was something about the way he looked at her. It was almost as if he hated her. But for whatever reason, James didn't mention it, his eyes slid over to his boyfriend instead.

"And as for you, what the hell do you have to say for yourself?" He demanded. Kieran simply arched an eyebrow in return, saying nothing as he concentrated on the narrow, twisting country road. "You know, the petrol in the back? Who needs that many petrol cans in their backseat?" He asked. "Rob a petrol station? Planning a little arson?" He continued.

"I was making a delivery to the camp when I felt him breach the perimeter." He finally answered, jerking his head towards Darius.

"Ah, a camp, huh?" He asked. "Like with small children roasting marshmallows or nudists?"

Alina choked again, coughing. "Nudists? A camp of nudists, seriously?"

James was nodding his head sagely. "Oh yeah, got to watch out for those nudists. They're amassing everywhere, you know."

"Jesus, I still can't believe someone put up with you long enough to become your boyfriend." She said, shaking her head.

"That is just rude. I see why you did so well in business, you have to be a bitch for that too I bet."

"James!" Kieran barked; startling Alina who squeezed Darius's hand harder than she meant to. He didn't pull away, just gave her a comforting smile, and squeezed back. Kieran sighed. "The camp is where my people live, what's left of the Fae." A silence fell over them as James and Alina were forced to face the truths they had just learned about the supernatural world. She just barely caught the sign that told her they were 62 kilometers from Galway. At least she had a vague idea about where they were now. If they were lucky, Darius could talk them out of whatever trouble they seemed to be in with the Fae and then Alina could get them a ship out of Galway. First, they'd have to find him some clothes that actually fit. All Kieran had in his car was a pair of sweats and an old raincoat. Neither of things were a good fit on Darius's much broader physique.

It wasn't long and Kieran was slowing the Land Rover down in front of a quaint, grey-stoned cottage. It was the only dwelling she had seen for miles. It was surrounded by an endless sea of thick, emerald green fields. The only exception to this was a raised ring of white stone to the right of the cottage. Kieran guided the car into the gravel drive, parking a few feet away from the cobble steps leading to the front door.

"This doesn't really look like a camp." She stated, sighing in relief when James hopped out, leaving her to rub the numbness from her legs.

"I hate to say it, but I have to agree with her, babe." James said, groaning as he stretched his long arms over his head to crack his back.

"That's because you're looking but you do not see." Kieran slid out of the driver's side, coming to stand in front of them. "Close your eyes." He said softly. James immediately closed his eyes, but Alina hesitated, she hadn't forgotten how he first looked at her. She glanced over at Darius who gave her an encouraging nod. When her eyes slid shut, she felt two of Kieran's fingers on her forehead. He tapped twice and a tingling sensation spread from the crown of her head to the center of her chest. "Now open your eyes."

CHAPTER TWO

Light danced across the tents set up in the middle of the white stone ring, throwing shadows across the fairy camp. There were maybe two dozen tents, set up with generators and clotheslines. Glittering blue, green, even one pair of purple eyes, shone out from inside the makeshift homes. One by one, families began to emerge. Most of the people were tall and slender with fine, angular features and sharp, shimmering eyes. Some had fine, silvery blonde hair that hung in straight planks framing their face while others had an untamable head of wild, fiery crimson curls. Very few of the people gathered around them had the same coloring or the shorter, stockier frame of Kieran, in fact, James seemed to almost fit in better with his boyfriends' people.

While she was admiring their ethereal beauty, Alina noticed as they started to whisper amongst themselves, casting fearful, distrusting glances. They seemed to be solely looking at her. One older, silver haired man even spat in her direction. "Darius…" She said, stepping gratefully into his embrace. "I-I don't understand."

The first time since the cave, he looked uneasy. "Neither do I." She tucked her head under his chin as Kieran barked something in Gaelic. A stunning red-haired woman stepped through the parting crowd and they seemed to argue for a moment, the conversation growing more heated between them before she finally jerked her head towards the stone cottage behind them and stormed back towards the center of camp, her emerald green skirt swishing around her legs.

Kieran grabbed James by the elbow, steering him towards the cottage. "Follow me. I have to take you to the Tiarna."

"Yeah, are we going to talk about the fact that apparently they can turn invisible?" He asked. "Or what the fuck a Tiarna is? Or how the hell you ended up so short, babe?"

Kieran didn't seem fazed by the rapid questions. "They weren't invisible, this place is protected by Fae magic, it's why they've gathered here. I don't take after them much. I have the least amount of The Blood of anyone here." He said and stopped them before the brightly painted red door. "And the Tiarna is what we call our king. He's my great-uncle."

Before anyone of them could think about knocking, the door creaked open and under its arch stood a hunched and wizened older man with one gnarled hand curled over the corner of the door frame. His white hair hung in thin, uneven clumps over his scalp, framing his long, angular face. Glittering jade shone from sunken eyes and stared right into Alina's heart. At least, that's how it felt to her, like he knew everything that she was, everything that she had ever thought, with that one shared glance.

"Hm." He hummed long and deep. "You had better bring them inside, Ellylldan." He said in a voice that was light and raspy and turned to hobble back into the cottage.

"Ellylldan?" James asked incredulously. "That wasn't a real word, it can't have been."

Alina noticed a light flush dusting Kieran's face and neck. "That's my true name, my Fae name." He answered and ushered them through the doorway.

James scoffed. "Well, you better not expect me to use it, or be able to pronounce it, or even remember it, because I'm telling you now babe, not going to happen."

"Yeah, please don't use it." He shot back and led them through a darkened hall into garishly lime green painted parlor. Kieran's great-uncle was already sitting in the only armchair in the room, gnarled hands loosely grasping the knobby handle of a wooden cane. On his middle finger, rested an intricately carved silver ring, though Alina couldn't make out any of the carvings beyond the Claddagh, and at its center rested a large, emerald green jewel that shone in the sunlight. As she stared, it became clear that it wasn't the sun causing it to glow, there was a light from within the jewel, it was dim but mesmerizing as it swirled around the center of the jewel.

"Sit, sit. I believe we have much to discuss, don't we?" He asked. "After all, my nephew dared to bring you here even though it's treason."

"Treason?!" James fell the rest of the way onto the cushion he had been aiming for. "Kieran, you lying bastard, you said we had to come here because we were trespassing or some shite."

"You weren't trespassing, just him." He said and nodded at Darius who had folded himself down awkwardly onto a footstool. "And her. She's not welcome in our territory. That's what he means. It was treason to bring her here." He explained.

Alina perched on the edge of a cushion, hugging her arms around her legs. "You owe me an explanation. I haven't done *anything,* but those people out there look at me like I'm a murderer!"

"You are." The old man said. "Or as good as one in any case."

"Then you can at least tell me what the hell that means." She said, starting to lose her patience. "I haven't hurt anyone."

"Haven't you?" He questioned. "You don't think that word of what you done has spread?"

"What am I supposed to have done besides free Darius from a life of enslavement and experimentation?" She asked, starting to get upset. She left the life she built for herself to help him and these people were treating her as if she were as bad as the ones that imprisoned him.

"You-" he jabbed his gnarled finger at her. "You

paid for the technology that put our people at risk. *All* our people, not just him and his. Witch-hunters," he spat the word. "They've been after us for years and now they suddenly have the technology to seek us out? They see through our magic, crush our defenses, and take our children. And for what? Well, you've already answered that yourself, for a life of experimentation and enslavement. They always thought our magic was the key to solving their mortality, they never stopped to question if they should have it."

Alina's heart was beating too loudly. How could nobody else hear it when it was the loudest thing in the room? It was all she could hear.

"Alina? Lina!" Darius's voice finally breached through her haze of panic.

"Are you trying to tell me that they took the money that I donated, and they-they did what? Made weapons?" She asked somewhat hysterically. "They told me that money was for his enclosure and further medical advancements that would change..." She trailed off. "Oh my God, they made weapons."

"The Titan Corporation has men in Ireland. They came four nights ago to Ballinderreen, a few of our people have homes there, and they took their children. They hit Kinvarra two days ago and Doolin just last night. It's why our people have started to gather here, there's safety in numbers." Kieran told them.

"Shit, they're taking kids?" James asked. "What

do those evil bastards want with the kids?"

"Not all of them." The old man said. "Aoife and Arits, twins, and the first among us to be born with wings in centuries. They were taken right out of their beds. Oren could cure the sick and Eldan could turn himself invisible."

"Uh, news flash, but everyone out there can turn themselves invisible." James pointed out but Kieran was shaking his head.

"I told you, they weren't invisible. It was just a glamour placed over the fairy circle." Kieran said.

"Look, I'm sorry that some of your children were taken, but if Titan used my money to make weapons, then I don't understand how this is somehow my fault." Alina said.

"They had sensors with them that could see through our strongest glamour." The old man said. "Or do you honestly believe they had that before your generous donation?"

"Okay." She buried her face in her hands, laughing humorously. "It's all my fucking fault. I get it. I gave them money and they used it to-to find your people and take your children." Her shoulders began to shake as her body was wracked by sudden sobs, tears slipping through her fingers. Her chest ached as her thoughts turned towards the children, who would no doubt be facing the same future as Darius had, albeit most likely less public.

Darius's broad, warm palm covered the small of her back, rubbing soothing circles as she cried. "Do you know where these men took the children?" He asked.

The old man tipped his head in a nod. "They have a headquarters outside of Cork, but there's too many of them. There's no way to get in, not when they can see through our glamour. Maybe if we strike when the moon is high..." He hummed thoughtfully.

"Uh...This is just off the top of my head, but there is this thing called The Police, or the Garda like you call them here." James said.

"Oh, shut *up*." Alina croaked. "They're a rich corporation who know a lot of powerful people. Trust me, they're untouchable."

Darius smiled sheepishly. "Not untouchable, I have bested them many times, and just recently on the ocean. Many years ago, our people had an alliance, I will honor it." He said. "I will go to this fortress of men and retrieve your children."

The old man's lips curled into a sneer. "I would not trust you enough to pass through these lands unattended, much less with the lives of our children."

Alina peaked through her fingers to look between the two of them, the old man seemed to have hit a nerve. Darius wouldn't meet his eyes, instead, he turned shamefaced towards the window. She wiped at her cheeks. "There has to be something we can do. This is all my fault, I-I have to fix it. I have to." She begged.

The old man pushed himself to his feet, fingers curling around the knobbed top of his cane. When he spoke, he addressed Kieran. "They can stay one night. In the main house, I don't want them around the others. When the sun rises, I want you to escort them to the Dublin port. They can leave our lands from there, *all* of them."

"Yes, Uncle." Kieran said obediently and the old man shuffled out of the parlor.

James released a huge rush of air from his lungs. "Shite! Did we just get banished? Does this mean I can't come to see you anymore, babe?" He asked.

Kieran ignored him, pushing himself up. "I'll show you to the guest room. James can stay with me."

"Oh yay, because you've been such a charming, thoughtful boyfriend all day." James mumbled under his breath. "Maybe I wanted to stay with the princess and her jovial jock."

"Shut up, James. Everything's always a joke to you, well, this isn't." Kieran said. He sounded exhausted, his brow was furrowed, and the corners of his mouth were pulled into a frown that seemed to age him. James angled his face away from the group; even with the small amount of time they spent together, Alina could see through his aloof attitude, and while she liked to gripe at him, she hated the sheen of tears building in his eyes. She reached out, squeezing his arm, trying not to be upset when he shook her off.

Kieran stopped outside of brightly painted, pastel yellow door. "This will be your room tonight. I'll bring you something to eat later. Don't try to leave this room unless you want to find yourself in even more trouble." He told them and grabbed James by the elbow, steering him farther down the hall.

"Right, let's see how our prison cell looks." She said and pushed open the door. As far as guest rooms went, this one looked like it was decorated by someone's grandmother. Floral wallpaper, a pink and white quilt covering the double bed, and crooked paintings of vases of exotic looking flowers. Darius closed the door behind them and walked to the bed, sinking down onto it, the bedframe squeaked under his weight but managed to hold. She stood beside the closed door and watched him. She hadn't seen him look so unhappy since the night she saw him in his enclosure at the lab.

She walked until she stood in front of him, dropping to her knees on the plush, pink rug. She settled her hands on the tops of his knees, peering up into his dark green eyes. "Darius, there's something you're not telling me. He has a reason to hate me, why does he seem to hate you?"

He sighed heavily, taking one of her hands from his leg and intertwining their fingers. "Centuries ago, my people had an alliance with the Fae." He explained. "Ireland was once tormented by the Fomori, you would call them water demons." He added, noticing her confusion. "They lived and hunted in the deep depths of lakes and oceans; Balor was their king. The Fae had lived, not so much in peace, but in compromise with the Fomori and other such supernatural creatures since they came into being, but Balor was wicked."

"What happened?" She asked, resting her chin on his knee.

"Balor killed enough mortals for the mortals to take notice." He said. "The early Celtic people began to create tales about the creatures that inhabited their land, and they began to fight back, only, they didn't discriminate what kind of creature they killed. The Fae were mischievous, but they didn't kill humans in droves like the Fomori did, the humans didn't care. The Fae knew that the only way to stop the slaughter was to go into hiding for a few generations, until fact became myth and legend, but Balor didn't want to hide from the humans."

"They went to war, didn't they?" She asked once Darius had paused.

"Yes. But they were fighting on two fronts, for the humans were still killing anything they deemed as different from themselves. The Fae couldn't defeat Balor's army and defend their people from the mortals, so they called upon my people for aid. At that time, we dragon shifters were facing our own problems on the mainland, I believe you call it Norway now." He said. "The humans were beginning to take more notice of our flying, they were becoming more organized, more dangerous. They invented weapons that could be shot into the sky, rip our wings. I was only a small child then, but I remember when their people came to mine for aid."

"And your people didn't help them," she finished for him.

"No, they did not. My grandfather didn't want to risk our people flying over such long distances, not over the human settlements encroaching on our lands. He thought it best if our own people went into hiding, so we retreated into the cave systems, it became illegal to shift into our other forms." He explained. "So, we did not answer their call for aid. We got some news over the years and heard that the Fae and Fomori had killed each other in the war. I had no idea there had been survivors, but these people here...They are weak. There looks to be hardly any of The Blood left in them, they must have interbred with the humans."

"The Blood?" She asked. "Kieran mentioned the same thing earlier."

"The Blood is what we call our magic. Interbreeding with humans dilutes it." He explained. "That is why you have abilities but cannot shift. You have some of The Blood, Alina, but diluted over time."

She squeezed his hand. "I'm sorry, this must be difficult for you to be here, but it's not fair for him to blame you. You said yourself that you were just a child at the time. You shouldn't be held accountable for what your grandfather did."

"Thank you, Lina love, but they were my

people. I must take responsibility for their wrongs." He said firmly. "I must speak with the Tiarna again in the morning. I cannot fix what has happened in the past, but I can help them get their children back."

She surged up, pressing their lips together. "Me too." She mumbled against his lips, pulling away just enough to speak properly. "My money made this possible. I need to be able to undo what I did." She told him.

A large, warm hand cupped the side of her face, the rough pads of his fingers scraping pleasantly against her scalp. "Then it seems as if you and I have much to atone for." He said and brought their mouths together again. She gasped as his touch awakened something inside her, warmth radiated from the center of her chest, spreading until her whole body felt electric. Her lips parted beneath his, her eyes fluttered closed against his dark, wanting gaze. She pushed up from her knees with her toes, pressing their mouths more firmly together, pulling that rumbling growl that she loved so much from deep in Darius's chest.

Darius dropped his hand, curling it around her hip instead, using the leverage to hoist her up and into his lap. He pulled back just far enough to swipe his tongue over her bottom lip and then he was kissing her fully, teeth nipping her lips, tongue delving inside her mouth. She had to press both hands against his chest to get him to pull away so she could speak. "Darius," she started, somewhat breathlessly. "We can't-I mean, we can't get too worked up. We can't have sex in someone's guest room." She hissed.

"No, we can't." He agreed and laid back on the bed, adjusting them until they were both laying on their sides, facing each other. He kissed her tenderly then, one hand cradling the side of her face as their tongues curled together languidly. His kiss was softer now, less urgent, moving from her mouth until he was brushing his lips against her temple. "Sleep, Lina, we will atone for our mistakes at dawn." And as if his whispered words were a spell, the exhaustion that had settled deep in her bones overtook her, sending her into a deep, comfortable sleep.

CHAPTER THREE

The gentle rapping at the bedroom door woke Alina from her peaceful sleep. For a moment, panic took hold of her as she gazed around the unfamiliar room, until she remembered the events of the last few days. She slid out from under Darius's heavy arm and pulled the door open a crack. Kieran stood in the threshold, he was dressed similarly as he was the day before and held a small bundle of clothes in his arms. He had dark circles under his tired blue eyes, his curly hair unwashed and falling limply around his face.

"I thought you might like a change of clothes before we left. These should fit you both." He said.

She stood up straight from her natural morning slouch, squaring her shoulders. "There's been a change of plans. We're going to speak with the Tiarna again."

"You can't." Kieran said. "He's already spoken."

"I wasn't asking you. I was telling you." She told him, breaking out into her boardroom voice, the one that usually earned her the flattering title of 'Bitch'. "We're going to meet with him after we've had breakfast, so you had better go and tell him to expect us."

Kieran's eyes narrowed on her, but he didn't say a word, just thrust the clothes at her, and spun on his heel, stalking back down the hallway. She shook her head, pulling the door shut behind her. She dropped the pile of clothes on Darius's head. "Wakey! Wakey!" She sung, smiling to herself as she watched him flail to get his head out from under the clothes.

He hummed, scraping a hand through his tousled, burgundy hair. "What time is it?" He asked.

"I'm not sure." She peered through the window curtain. "But the sun is just beginning to rise." She rifled through the pile of clothes, peeling off her dirty shirt to put on the rather beautiful deep purple tunic that Kieran had found for her with a pair of black, leather leggings. "Kieran brought us a change of clothes." She explained. "Even though what I really want is a shower." She watched Darius did through the pile and pull on a faded pair of jeans and a tight green t-shirt, although everything usually seemed tight on Darius. "I told him to set up another meeting with the Tiarna. He didn't seem very happy about it."

"I don't imagine that he would have." He said. "He doesn't seem to have a good relationship with his uncle."

Alina hummed in agreement. "Do you think it's because of James?" She asked.

"He can be very trying, but I don't know why that alone would make the Tiarna hate him." Darius said, his brow furrowing in confusion.

"No, no, not that he's an asshole just because he's, you know, he's a man." She explained.

Darius tilted his head, looking like a confused Labrador. "What else would he be?" She smiled despite herself, leaning up so she could kiss him. She felt his answering smile against her lips. "What was that for, my Lina?"

"Nothing, I just forget how kind you are sometimes." She said and grabbed his hand, lacing their fingers together. "Let's find the kitchen. I'm tired of waiting for someone to feed me."

***

They found Kieran in the dining room, setting a table with plates of fruit, breads, cheese, and cold cut meat. He sighed when he saw them. "You aren't supposed to be wandering on your own."

"We're starving. What kind of breakfast is this?" She asked.

"You can complain about it to my uncle. I only do what I'm told." He groused. His sour expression only lifting when James appeared in the doorway, his artfully tousled bottle-blond hair looking especially mused.

"Food!" He cheered and tried to snag an entire tray of sliced cheese. Kieran caught the other end before it could leave the table and the two began to play a game of tug of war for the tray. Alina was happy to see James's eyes looked much brighter than they had the night before, probably due to the red mark she could see peeking up behind the collar of his garish yellow and green shirt.

"Have a good night then James?" She asked, laughing when in surprise, he dropped his corner of the tray, scattering sliced cheese across the nicely set table.

"Haha, hilarious, like I don't remember what you two get up to behind closed doors." He said, filching a slice of cheese from the mess on the table. Whatever she was going to say next died in her throat when Kieran's uncle shuffled into the room, clearing his throat.

"Sit." He commanded and Alina, Darius, and Kieran found themselves instantly lowering themselves into a seat as if compelled by his voice. James still hovered over the table, stuffing his pockets with food. Kieran was staring at him like the man had grown a second head. When he noticed their staring, he swallowed the mouthful of food he was chewing.

"Don't mind me, I'll be quiet as a mouse." He said.

"I told you to sit." The Tiarna said but it came out almost like a question.

"Oh yeah, mate, but I'm not actually part of that little suicide squad there, I'm just here for the food and then I'll be out of your way." James tried to explain.

"I said sit!" The old man roared, and James set down his handful of food.

"All right, keep your trousers on, Jesus." He muttered and plopped into an empty chair beside

Kieran.

The Tiarna stood, hunched over the table, his middle finger tapping softly on the knotted handle of his cane, sending the light dancing in his ring. "Someone explain to me what this charade is about? You were supposed to leave this morning and be grateful for it."

Alina spoke first when it became apparent none of the boys were going to. "We respectfully decline your offer for transportation to the port. We can all agree that this is my fault."

"Lina-" Darius started to protest.

"I gave the funding to the people that attacked your family. That was all me, my fault." She pressed on. "But you can't expect me to leave this island without doing something to fix it." She glanced at Darius, smiling sadly. "We all have a lot to atone for and you can't do this without our help. Darius is the muscle and I've worked with them for months. I know their security protocols, I know their tech, and if you let me, I think I can get us into that building."

"Even if we were willing to look past your failings, what makes you think we would ever work with the likes of him?" He asked. "His grandfather-"

"He is not his grandfather! You cannot hold him responsible for something that happened when he was a child." She argued. "Please, let us help you."

The Tiarna stared down at them with his glittering lavender eyes, the silence only broken by

James's loud whispering. "Babe, I definitely didn't volunteer for this." And Kieran's answering hiss to silence him.

Finally, the Tiarna tipped his head in a nod. "Then on behalf of my people, we will accept your aid."

Alina's answering smile was genuine. "Thank you, thank you so much. I swear we'll get your children back for you. Let's start over. I'm Alina, that's Darius, and James."

"Yeah, still didn't volunteer my time, sweetheart."

"My name is Midhir Fairy King of Éire, Uniter of the tribes of Connacht, Leinster, Munster, and Ulster, descendant of the Slayer of Balor, the son of Moren, Chief of Bards." He said and lifted his hand that bore the ring.

"Right... Very impressive." She said dumbly.

Darius rose, hand fisted over his heart. "Darius, son of Daere, Chief of Huntsmen. I vow to you my service until you deem the honor of my people restored."

"What fucking year did we drop into? Am I dead?" James asked, yelping when Kieran smacked the back of his head. "Ow! You arsehole. What the hell was that for?"

"To prove you aren't dead." Kieran answered simply.

"Enough." Midhir said. "You will still have to stay inside this house until I have explained your presence to the rest of my people. I fear they will not take to you as kindly as I have."

"Oh, is that what you did?" James asked. "Ow! Quit hitting me." He whined when Kieran gave him another smack to the back of the head.

"Kieran, you will come with me. The people trust your judgement." Midhir said and Kieran rose, taking his arm to help walk his uncle out the door. "Remember, you must stay indoors until I tell you otherwise."

***

And that is how Alina and James found themselves perched on the top of a dining room chair, straining to look out of the upstairs window as Kieran and Midhir gathered their people below. There were more of them since they arrived yesterday, a little over two dozen, very few of them were children. Some of them were dressed in long tunics and leggings, their long hair braided intricately away from their face, while others looked like what Alina would describe as ordinary working families. One woman even sported a bob and a power suit.

Darius sat on the bed behind them, shaking his head at their antics. "You shouldn't be spying after the Tiarna was gracious enough to accept our aid." He scolded.

James scoffed. "What am I supposed to kiss his arse because he's nice enough to *allow* us to risk our lives for *his* people? I don't think so, mate. Thanks for lumping me in with you lot, by the way, how'd you know I had so much fun the last time I almost died that I'd like to try it again?" He asked.

Darius hummed thoughtfully. "Perhaps I thought that you cared about your lover and that you would care about what happened to his people."

James was quiet for a moment. "Well, how could I turn you down? I am very good at hitting people in the head with heavy objects."

"Sh!" Alina interrupted, cracking the window open. "They're talking." She said and she and James leaned closer, tilting their heads to try to catch what they were saying to the crowd.

"Shite, I can't hear a word." James complained. "But those don't look like happy faces." And they weren't, as far as Alina could make out, the faces in the crowd varied from mildly displeased to openly hostile. The red-haired woman from early was pushing her way to the front of the crowd, she seemed to be the most vocal about her disapproval. Her wild hair whipped in the wind, the silver bangles she wore sliding up her arms as she gestured violently. She seemed to be rousing the others and soon displeased faces turned into arguing mouths that formed a dull roar of noise coming from below them.

Midhir moved suddenly, banging his cane once upon the white stone where he stood. The vibration immediately silenced the mob and whatever he said next seemed to appease them. All except the red-haired woman who looked the embodiment of fury as she stormed away from the crowd and into the swaying field beyond the camp. The rest of the crowd began to slowly disperse, and Kieran began to help Midhir back towards the cottage.

"Well, she sure looked like a bundle of sunshine, didn't she?" James asked, hopping down from the chair. "That was way less exciting then I thought it'd be."

"He was down there telling them who we are and what we're doing here. What did you think was going to happen?" She asked.

"I was hoping for a fist fight, I guess, or maybe for the geezer to whack someone with that stick of his. Now that would have been a show." He said.

"I hope the geezer you're referring to isn't the King of the Fae, by who's generosity has you fed and clothed and housed, and who happens to be my great-uncle." Kieran said from the doorway to the bedroom, a fond smile stretched over his lips.

"Course not, I was talking about that funny looking short bloke he was standing with." James quipped, bounding over to his boyfriend. He hung off his shoulders, grinning up at him. "Are you here to entertain me?"

"I'm here to make sure you don't offend someone and get stabbed." He corrected. He tore his eyes away from the blond hanging off his shoulders to address Alina and Darius. "My uncle is having a meeting tonight with our warriors, he wants you to join. Until then you're free to do as you like.

There's a town not far from here and hiking paths if you fancy a walk. I wouldn't linger in the camp, not everyone there trusts your offer to help."

"What do you mean?" She asked.

"Some of them think you might still be working for Titan, spying for them." He said.

"I guess we can't just show up and expect them to trust us... We'll have to prove it to them." She said and Darius got up to join her, kissing the side of her face.

"They will see how pure your heart is, Lina." He whispered.

James gagged. "Jesus, get me out of here before they start waxing poetry to each other." He jumped, Kieran's strong arms catching him and carrying him bridal style out of their room.

Alina angled her body towards Darius's affectionate hands, standing on her toes so she could press their mouths together in a soft kiss. "Do you want to explore the town or go for a walk?"

"I am not sure if venturing into the village would be a good idea, my Lina, news of my escape may have already reached this place." He said apologetically.

She smiled against his lips as she pressed them together again. "I was hoping you'd say that. I've never been to Ireland; I was hoping to actually see a little bit of it while we're here."

His large hands cupped her hips, squeezing them gently. "How about I pack us a lunch and you can meet me outside. I think I remember a place near here that I would like to share with you."

She grinned, pecking his lips one more time. "Deal."

Outside the cottage, it was difficult to hang onto the happiness she had felt inside with Darius. Solemn and displeased faces greeted her as she walked through the camp and towards the hiking trail Kieran pointed out. Out here it was impossible to forget what these people had gone through, were still going through. Families stayed grouped together in tight units, only the necessities brought with them to their makeshift home. Even their children were kept under a tight leash, parent's jerking them back if they tried to wander to far. She wanted to help them so they could return to their real homes. They shouldn't have to live in a city of tents just because they were afraid.

She didn't try to talk to them, it would probably only upset them further. They didn't see her as someone who could help yet, they only saw her as a threat. She got to the edge of the camp, stepping over the white stones that encircled it when her path was suddenly blocked by the beautiful, red-haired woman. Her hair was living fire, eyes as vibrant emerald as the ring that the king wore, she looked beautiful, and dangerous. Up close, she noticed a scattering of freckles across the bridge of her nose and upper cheeks.

"You have no right to be here. This is our land and the king never should have let a snake like you into the grass." She said, her accent thick as the words dripped out of her mouth. She had changed out of the skirt Alina had seen her in yesterday, she wore a bright green colored belted tunic instead, but what really drew the eye was the knives she had strapped up her inner and outer thighs.

"And like I told your king; I need to fix the wrongs that I've done. I know you don't trust me, but I really am here to help." She said.

"You may be able to fool an old, senile man, with your honeyed words and your doe eyes but don't even try it with me. It's like trying to squeeze blood from stone, darlin', it's not going to happen." She said. "I can't go against the word of the king, but the moment you betray us, it will be my blade that kills you."

"Then lucky for me, I have no intention of betraying you." She said brusquely and shoved past her, knocking their shoulders together. She'd have to tell James that if she ended up with a dagger in the back, to start the investigation with that one.

CHAPTER FOUR

They followed the trail through dewy fields, shoes squelching in the mud as they passed patches of knee-deep grass. Their path led them downhill and into the cool shadows of the north facing slopes, the sun bathing them in its warmth whenever they stepped out of the shade. The air was damp and cold, and as they walked, they were under constant threat of the heavy, dark cloud following above them, laden with moisture. The after-noon sun was high in the sky, peeking between dark clouds when they crested the last hill, casting rolling shadows down the valley below them.

Alina stopped on the hilltop, admiring the spring fed pool of water that gathered at the feet of the castle ruins in the center of the vale. The castle itself was in complete disrepair, its ceilings crumbled and walls eroding under the heavy weight of time. The ivy climbing its towers curled around the stone like filigree and wildflowers grew between piles of fallen stone. It was still beautiful, even as natured reclaimed it.

"I must admit it was more impressive when I

was here last." Darius said.

"I think it's stunning." She said and nudged him with her shoulder. "Let's go down, I'd love a closer look. You can give me a tour." So, they walked down the slope and into the sleepy meadow. Alina had her arms outstretched; fingers spread wide to touch the tips of the soft, green grass. She felt her eyes close, letting the energy swirling around them pull her towards the castle. There was power at work here, it was palpable in the air and swept goosebumps across her skin. She came back into awareness of herself when Darius wrapped his fingers around her elbow, tugging her through the stone arch way and into the great, fallen entrance hall.

"This way. I still remember the way to the courtyard. When I was a child, there was a tree that grew there but it was so much more than that." He told her.

"Darius, that doesn't make any sense." She complained, her head twisting and turning to peer down passages and spiral, stone staircases. "Can't we explore inside first?"

"You'll understand when you see it." He promised.

"Darius, we don't even know if it will be there. The tree might be dead by now." She said. "Besides, I think it can wait until-" The rest of the sentence died in her mouth as they passed under another arch into the courtyard. The garden was overgrown, the plants grew thick and wild without someone to cultivate them, but all that fell away as she focused on what was growing in the center of the courtyard. It looked like a hazel tree, but she had never seen one with smooth, ivory bark. Its wide, lush leaves were bright emerald green and the veins pulsed with a pale, cosmic glow. She knelt before it in the tall, summer grass and let herself become washed in the pure life energy that pulsated all around her.

She didn't know how many minutes passed before she sighed and pushed herself to her feet. She felt more at peace and well-centered than as long as she could remember. She spied Darius watching her, lingering at the edge of the courtyard. When she walked back to him, she offered him a grateful smile.

"I don't know what this place is but thank you. I think I needed to be here," she told him.

He pushed a piece of her hair back behind her ear, "I know."

"What is this place?" She asked.

"This is the essence of the island, its spirit. It's impossible to find except for the few who have already been in its presence," he explained.

She grabbed his hand, tugging him back towards the archway of the castle. "Let's go back in, I think we have a little longer before we have to start heading back." She let her fingers trail over the rough-hewn stone as they wandered deeper inside that ruined place. They passed through another tall arch, still showing fragments of the filigree that had been carved into the stone in sweeping, twirling designs. A pale sun sent its rays of light across the misty sky and through the tall, narrow windows that opened to the courtyard. Beams of yellow light fell across the stone floor, worn smooth over the years by hundreds of treading feet.

"What did this room used to be?" She asked.

"They used to dance in here." Darius said. "Sometimes, the music would play all night and into the early light of dawn. The Fae loved music and dancing most of all."

"Would you dance with me?" She asked.

His answering smile was reflected in his eyes. "We have no music."

"Don't you dare be boring." She told him, wrapping her arms around his neck, their torsos pressed together. Darius curled his arms around her waist, bringing them impossibly closer. With soft, confident steps, he began to sway them in a circle around what was left of the dance floor. She laid her head on his chest, letting the strong thrum of his heart lull her away.

She was in the veil between awake and asleep when she heard the music. It didn't start out quietly and then crescendo, it just was. It was loud, the archaic beat of drums, the swell and ebb of a string instrument she recognized but couldn't quite place. Darius was gone. She could still feel the heat of his arms around her waist, but he was gone, and around her couples twirled across a firelit dance floor. There was only one other figure standing still among the graceful dancers. She stood across the dance floor, a torch on the wall bathing her face in wiggling shadows.

The deep purple of her gown glittering like a nebula, the tumultuous dark curls of her hair spilling down her back and shoulders, and her eyes were two orange flames, locked on Alina. Pink lips twitched up in a secret smile and she brought one pale finger to her lips, shhhing.

There was a sensation like a tug behind her naval and suddenly she was back in Darius's strong arms, her ear pressed over his beating heart. It was on the tip of her tongue. She was going to tell him what she saw, but then she thought of the woman and her secret smile. She lifted her head from his chest. "Kiss me." She said instead.

Darius kissed her; their swaying stilled in the ruined palace bathed in golden light. It was a sweet, chaste kiss. One that filled her heart with warmth. It was probably the best kissed they ever shared.

"Do you remember when I said we couldn't have sex in a strangers house?" She asked.

He hummed. "I think I recall you mentioning that."

"Well, I don't think that applies here." She said cheekily and tilted her head up to meet his kiss. She can't help the pitiful moan that escapes her lips when he tilts his head and licks at the seam of her closed mouth. She's been wanting to kiss him, properly kiss him for hours, but she'd rather not do it with an audience, particularly James.

Her hands fisted in the fabric of his borrowed shirt, just the press of his lips against hers, the heat of his body seemed to fill the emptiness she had felt for years. It was a part of her that knew he was out there somewhere, waiting for her. Their mouths moved to together, not as desperate as the first time they made love, but softly, exploring each other. He nipped her bottom lip, his tongue finally delving inside her mouth, sliding over hers. His big hands were cupping her face, thumbs stroking up the arches of her cheeks, while their teeth clicked to together as they grew more heated.

There was something filthy about kissing this way, their tongues sliding together, breath panted into one another's mouths, every sensation was wet and slick and hot, and it made desire pool inside her belly. They separated with a soft smack as their mouths parted, Darius's arms dropped to her waist, squeezing the curve of her hips in his overly large hands. He stroked up her body, the soft material of her borrowed tunic tickling her sides as it bunched between his fingers.

She leaned against his strong torso and threaded her fingers into his wild auburn hair, pulling him in for one more kiss. His breath was hot against her skin, his mouth rough as he kissed her like he meant to claim her. He ducked his head, working his mouth across her throat, scraping his teeth lightly across her pulse point. She tugged gently at her hair, making a soft noise of need. "Darius, please..." She begged, not fully knowing what she was begging for. "We don't have much time before we have to go."

"Sh, let me take care of you, my Lina." He whispered against the hollow of her throat and took her hands, prying them from his hair. He drew her off the stone dance floor and into a little alcove that was overgrown with soft, leafy underbrush. He pulled her to lay across the floor and then stretched down beside her, his hands roaming, exploring the soft curves of her body overtop her tunic. One hand rested over the curve of her hip, the other settling on the mound of her breast. He flicked teasingly over her hardening nipple, finding the hem of her tunic and pulling it over her head.

He stared down at her, heated eyes taking in the revealed unblemished skin, glowing in the shards of sunlight trickling through the cover of mist. His fingers ghosted over her collarbone, tracing filigree down her sternum, his fingers fanning out as he cupped the mounds of her breasts. He ducked his head, pressing kisses one by one down the valley between her breasts while his fingers circled her nipples. Her breath was coming faster, little gasps leaving her parted lips, one shaking hand coming up to cup the back of his head as she arched into the touch of his lips.

Darius drew one of her nipples into his mouth

and she dug her teeth into her bottom lip, feeling her skin pebbling as he laved against her skin. He scraped his teeth across her nipple, pulling back until he could blow across her dampened skin, gooseflesh raising across her skin, wracking her body with shivers that traveled up the length of her spine. His warm hand skimmed her side as moved his head to pay equal attention to her other nipple until both were hard and pebbled under his gentle touch. He leaned back on his knees, pulling his shirt over his head, falling back down to bare the rest of her.

Cool, damp air misted over her newly revealed skin, but his hands slid down her bare thighs, igniting a fire under her flesh wherever he touched. His eyes drug over her bodying, taking in her narrow waist that flared into wide, curvy hips and creamy thighs. He leaned over her, pressing hot, open mouthed kisses down her sternum to her naval. She couldn't help the gasp that escaped her when his tongue circled the rim of her bellybutton.

"Darius," she breathed softly, curling her fingers into his hair.

He followed the curve of her body until her was pressing kisses into her inner thighs which had fallen open for him as he stretched out between her legs. There was no prelude, no word or warning as Darius suddenly scooted closer, his head pillowed between her thighs, and teased the tip of his tongue between her folds. His fingers curled around her thighs, forcing them further apart as he licked deeper inside her channel.

"Darius, oh fuck," she said at the sudden burst of sensation. Her fingers tightened painfully in his hair, nails scraping over his scalp.

With each swipe of his tongue, the heat pooling in her body grew and when he drew his tongue out to find her clit, circling it in slow, torturous sweeps, the heat inside her bloomed into her first orgasm. Her thighs were trembling under his solid grip, her fingers locked in his hair, her other hand grasping as her own throat, trying to control her quick breaths. When she finally regained her breath, she glanced down towards him, her cheeks burning with more than exertion when she saw him staring. His eyes were heated, pupils dilated, the muscles across his back and shoulders flexing when he pushed to his hands and knees to kiss her, sharing her taste.

He rose to his knees, leaning back on his calves as she fumbled with the fastening of his on his jeans. She finally got them unbuttoned, shoving them down his hips so she could wrap her hand around the length of his cock, giving him a slow, firm stroke. She smiled as Darius bucked his hips into her hand, chasing the friction. He gently batted her hand away, shuffling forward on his knees, bending over her outstretched body so he could kiss her. He moved his mouth insistently over hers, his tongue sweeping between her lips, rolling against her tongue. He bit softly at her reddened mouth as the thick head of his cock probed at her entrance.

One of his hands landed on her cheek, his thumb stroking her cheek as inch by inch he sank inside. Her nails pierced the skin of his back, his lips capturing her cry when he finally stopped. She could feel herself fluttering around him in the last fading throes of her receding orgasm. Darius didn't move, he waited, keeping them locked together, bodies pressed flush together as they were ignited in sweet, agonizing heat. He swept his thumb under her eyes, a fire and pulsing with a ruby glow.

"Beautiful." He told her. She dragged her nails down his spine, leaving a swirl of flames that sank into his heated skin. Darius braced his hands on either side of her head and slowly slid part way out of her, snapping his hips forward again. He set a brutal rhythm, encouraged by the pleased sounds, and pleading that escaped her lips. Their hips rolled together, Alina's back arching off the ground as a second orgasm tore through her. Her entire body was a light, a full body shiver wracked through her, spreading from her spine to the tips of her fingers and toes. So enthralled in her own bliss, she almost missed when Darius buried himself to the hilt and came, flooding her body with another pulse of warmth.

Darius was breathing hard against her neck, his muscles slowly relaxing after being stiff with exertion, when she laughed breathlessly. He lifted his head a little, straining to look at her. "I hope that's not a sign of my performance." He said gruffly.

"What? No, of course not. I was just thinking that...Well, I keep thinking that it can't be like every time but then we have sex again and it's just as good, better even." She tried to explain.

"What do you mean?" He asked.

"Nothing, nothing. I'm just happy, that's all I mean to say. I'm...I'm really happy." She said, feeling surprised to hear herself say it, but maybe more surprised to mean it. She picked a dried leaf from the tangled mess on the back of her head. "Maybe next time we could be indoors?" She asked with a little, tinkling laugh.

"I think that would be for the best." Darius agreed, trying to shake the leaves from his shirt before he pulled it over his head. They dressed in the companionable silence of two lovers that had known each other a lot longer than they had and when they were finished, they linked hands and walked away from the castle and its crumbling stone garden, towards the encampment at Killeeneen and what remained of the Fae people.

CHAPTER FIVE

The moon was hidden by a shroud of rolling, black clouds by the time they returned to the encampment. Alina was grateful for the flickering light of the Fae's bonfire, by the time nightfall had crept in, it was the only light they had to guide their return. Midhir had kept his word and gathered what Alina supposed was the last of his warriors. In reality, what this looked like was half a dozen, tall, silver-haired men sitting around the bonfire, passing around an amber colored bottle while they watched James tell, what Alina was sure was, a vulgar and completely fabricated story.

Kieran was standing at his uncle's side, arguing heatedly with the fiery, crimson haired woman that Alina had ran into earlier. She and Darius approached the group as James finished his story, sending the group of men into raucous laughter. James turned his quick grin on them, his entire face lighting up in delight as he took in their appearance. Alina held up her hand in warning. "Not a word, James, I mean it."

James reached past her ear and plucked a stray

leaf from her hair, his brow arching inquiringly. "Hm, now, I do wonder what the two of you have been doing all day. Let me just ask you one question, Lina-cakes, did you find that the walk there was easier than the walk back?"

She smacked at his hands as he tried to snatch another leaf off her. "I told you no comments!"

"Ow! Quit hitting me!"

"You big baby! Ow!"

Darius's arms encircled the two of them, squashing them both against his chest. "Could we perhaps cease the childish bickering in front of King Midhir and his warriors.?"

"He started it."

"She started it."

"Sorry," she finally said, clearing her throat awkwardly. "Could you let us go now?"

"I will be on my best behavior, mate." James assured him.

"That's not saying much." She said, yelping when he pinched her side in retaliation. "Hey!"

Darius squeezed his arms more tightly around them, squishing the air from their lungs. James broke first, tapping his fist against one of Darius's large biceps. "Uncle, uncle, I give. We'll behave, I swear."

"Thank you." He said and slowly released them, his eyes sparkling when he gave Alina one last, and far more gentle, affectionate squeeze.

"I'm glad some of us are in good humor." The flame-haired woman interrupted. "We're only here to discuss the fates of our missing children, after all."

The laughter and smiles around the firepit faded and Alina felt a white-hot stab of embarrassment and guilt slash through her. In the afternoon spent in the arms of her lover, she had almost forgotten the danger they were about to face, the danger that those poor children were in. *How could I be so selfish to forget?*

"Brigid speaks the truth; this night is not for revelry," Midhir spoke in a low voice, leaning for support on his knotted cane. The light from his ring flickered and blazed brilliantly in the firelight. The three of them lowered themselves into the last available seats around the firepit, Alina found herself uncomfortably squeezed between the last two men in her life.

"I've gathered you here this night to discuss the raid on Titan to recover our children. As most of you know, there will be a full moon tomorrow night. I believe we should attack then, when our power is strongest." There was a rumble of agreement amongst the men around her, but Alina couldn't help but voice her doubt.

"Attack?" She asked dubiously. "You can't just *attack* the Titan facility. They have security measures that you can't even imagine. We would need an entire army to get past the guards alone."

"This isn't New York City." Brigid interrupted hotly. "This isn't their corporation headquarters, it's just an outpost."

"Outpost or not, they're not stupid. You don't think they would have thought about local resistance? They knew that Darius and I were headed for Ireland and they damn well know that a handful of armed guards aren't going to restrain him." She stared earnestly at Midhir. "However many men you think there are, I guarantee you there's at least twice that, maybe more."

Brigid scoffed, angling her sharp eyes right through her. "Then what would you have us do? Because I didn't realize you were also a military tactician."

"Are you?" She asked her seriously, rising from her seat. "Are any of you? Your last war was a thousand years ago. Were any of you actually alive to see it?"

Brigid stood to meet her. "Just because we were born after The Great War doesn't mean we've not faced battle. Each one of my people has more fight in them and has seen more hardship then you could ever comprehend, including the wee ones." She spit into the ground at Alina's feet, but Alina had built her business in New York from the ground up, she was used to being intimidated.

She spoke to Brigid, not unkindly. "You may have trained, and sparred, and even fought with humans or creatures that I couldn't even imagine, but one on one? That's a world away from an actual battle, even I know that." She turned her eyes back on Midhir who was still slumped over in his chair. "If you order a direct attack on Titan, your people will be slaughtered, and when the public finds out about it, which they will, you will have given Titan everything they need to paint your people into monsters."

"Lina," Darius interrupted gently. "They would not be facing them alone; I would be with them. I could face legions of men. One outpost, no mattered how armed, would be no trouble for me."

A heavy sigh left her body, it was the sigh of a woman who could see the threads of fate pulling her closer and closer to bloodshed. "Darius," she said pleadingly. "You cannot turn into a fucking dragon in the middle of an Irish town, you just can't. The media has already turned us into a less flattering version of Bonnie and Clyde. Besides, we don't know what kind of weapons they've developed with my money, we don't know how many of them there are, and we don't even know if they're waiting for us. This is a *bad* idea."

"For the record, if anyone actually gives a shite," James glared pointedly at Kieran. "I'm with Linacakes, this is mad. I don't know how to stage a fucking attack and no offense, but it doesn't really seem like you lot know how to either."

"Silence." Midhir brought his cane down on the white stone beneath him with a crack. "I will hear what the outsider has to say."

"Right, uh, thanks." She mumbled and cleared her throat. "Let Darius and I go in first. We could pretend to turn ourselves in, all their attention would be on us. Once we're *inside* the outpost," she said pointedly, "Darius can transform and cause an even bigger diversion. That will draw everyone to us with Darius on the loose and then a small, quiet team can slip in, find the children, and get out. We'll need some kind of signal so we know when you've got them and then Darius can fly us out into the cloud coverage, and we can meet you back here at the safe house."

"You want us to rely entirely on you?" Brigid asked incredulously. "You were working with Titan not three months ago. How are we supposed to know that you aren't leading us right into a trap? No matter who you charm or how many beds you warm, *I* remember that it was you who armed the enemy. I wouldn't follow you anywhere."

"Brigid speaks the truth, as much as you claim to want to help, we can't trust you." Midhir said, using his cane to push himself to his feet. "We will attack the outpost tomorrow, while the moon is full." He spoke with finality.

"Uncle," Keiran began, looking uncertainly at Alina. "Maybe we should discuss this a little more. The outsiders make a good point, and I can't sit by and let you lead our people into a slaughter."

"Let me? Let me?!" Midhir raged towards him half a step, swinging his cane with a strength that Alina was surprised to see he possessed. Kieran made no move to defend himself from the blow, his eyes taking on a resigned kind of pain, and Alina was prepared to see him be struck across the face with the knotted end of the cane when James shot out his hand, fingers curling around the wood before it could strike his partner.

"I know your kind of a big deal around here, but I'd appreciate it if you didn't damage the goods. I'm only with him for his looks, you know." James said with a lascivious wink into Kieran's shocked face. His fingers released the cane and if fell to the earth with a dull thud. All Midhir's men were on their feet, some of them had long, curved steel blades pointed at him, one of them had a pistol pointed to the back of his tousled, bottle-blond head. He glanced around with the vague surprise of someone who could never take anything seriously, even his own eminent bodily harm. "Eh, so am I about to get executed or something? Because I think that's just a tad unfair, all I did was stop an old geezer from cracking my man's head open. Do I get a trial first at least? May-"

Midhir snatched up his cane, his face thunderous. "What are you, boy? Answer me!"

"What am I? Is this a joke?" He questioned, bringing his hands up in surrender. "I don't know what you're talking about! This entire place is a madhouse."

"James, darlin', how did you do that?" Kieran asked gently, his hand wrapping around his elbow, steering the other man to his side.

"How did I do *what*? I just grabbed the end of his stick, you know, I knew he whacked people with that thing. I knew it!"

"But how?" Kieran pressed.

"I don't fucking know; I have good reflexes, I guess. Why is this such a big fucking deal?" James asked.

"Because he swung with his ring hand." Kieran explained like that was supposed to answer their questions.

"And? He's like a hundred years old! A stiff breeze in the right direction could knock him off his feet. Ow!" He complained when Midhir slapped the side of his head, his ring glinting in the firelight. "You people have got to quit hittin' me!" He complained, his accent growing thicker as he rubbed the side of his head. "Okay, old man, I'll give you, you're stronger than you look."

Around them, the men had released the breath that they had been holding. Alina was clearly as lost in the significance of the ring as James was if Kieran's pale face was anything to go by. He carefully moved James's hand where it held the side of his head, examining the area around it. Color was finally returning to his cheeks when he addressed the rest of them. "He's fine. He's not hurt. He probably won't even bruise." He breathed the last part, his eyes sparkling in amazement as he studied his boyfriend. That look did not transfer to his uncle, who he turned his attention to next. "You could have killed him!"

"He is an outsider and now, a potential threat. He will not be going tomorrow night." Midhir said.

"Uncle, James doesn't know-"

"I have spoken, Ellylldan." He said firmly.

"Uncle, I will not go without him." Kieran said softly.

"So be it." Midhir answered.

"Right, this has been nice and dramatic, but would anyone care to explain what the fuck is going on?!" James asked, his voice raising the longer he spoke.

Brigid, who until that moment had been watching the goings on with a cat's eye interest, motioned gracefully to the glowing ring on Midhir's old, gnarled finger. "That is the ring of Croí." She explained. "In that ring is the power, the life, the *heart* of our people, the Fae. Since it was forged, it has never gone dark, and the Tiarna, the King of Fae, has always been its bearer. That ring grants the king extra strength in his time of need, he can call on the spirits of our people to aid him, to give him strength."

"So...what? He's got like one really strong arm then?" James asked. "Jesus, I guess you'd better remember to take that off before you have a wank."

"James!" Alina gasped, horrified and unable to help herself.

Before Kieran could cover his mouth and pull him to relative safety, Brigid had the edge of curved dagger pressed to the soft, white column of James's throat. "I'd speak with a little more respect to our king, if I were you. The point remains that you shouldn't have been able to stop his cane and seeing as he also hit you upside the head with his full strength, you should also be dead."

The delighted gleam that always seemed to exist there left James's eyes, his mouth lost its upturned smirk and tightened into a thin line. "Listen, love, I've been told my whole life what I should be. I am who I am, and I talk how I talk, but one thing I don't do is take threats. So, if you're going to kill me, then kill me, but I'm not going to grovel." Brigid studied him; her green, cat-like eyes bore straight into his. Whatever she saw in James in that moment seemed to appease her, and she lowered her dagger, stepping away from him with her skirt swishing around her ankles.

"You still aren't human." She said.

"Well, I'm not anything else either." He quipped.

"I don't care what he is or what he isn't." Midhir interrupted. "He is an outsider and he will not be trusted. Not on such an important night."

"Suit yourself, mate, I wasn't exactly volunteering to go anyway." James muttered.

"The woman will not be going either." He said and Alina glanced at Brigid, unable to believe that such a skilled warrior wouldn't be joining the king and his men, only to find her staring straight back at her. *Oh...*

"Darius and I go together. I know how badly you need him to help you. I'm not trying to be rude, but you know that you need him if you're going to have even a *chance*." She hissed. Helping the Fae recover their children had been her idea, she wasn't about to let them sideline her. "If I don't go, then Darius doesn't."

"Lina..." Darius began gently, but she turned to him before he could finish, catching the guilt in his expression.

It was as if a pit had been opened beneath her feet. She was falling, she had to be falling. "Darius, you can't be serious. We decided this together. You said we'd do this *together*." She pleaded. "What happened to restoring our honor? Or whatever the hell it was you said?"

"In completing this quest, I will restore honor to both of our names, but I must do this. Not only for you but for my people. This could repair our relationship with the Fae. An ally would not be something to take for granted in this age."

"I can't-I don't understand." And she didn't. She was still falling, now accompanied by roaring in her ears and a black shroud slowly cloaking her sight.

"I am sorry, My Lina, this is far too dangerous of a pursuit for you anyway." He said and she was vaguely aware of his lips pressing against the overheated skin on her forehead.

"Darius..." She pleaded one last time.

"I will regale you with tales of my victory upon my return." He promised, but how could he not see that she was falling?

"Take them to the cellar room." She heard Midhir say. "I want them secure while we plan our attack. They are not to be allowed to run loose among my people until our return."

"Yes, Tiarna."

"Wait, wait just a minute, cellar room? Are you locking us up? I am not going in some fucking cellar. Kieran!"

"Uncle, you can't possibly think that imprisoning them for two days is a fair treatment of our guests."

"Then you can join them!"

"Uncle!"

She heard this taking place, beyond her, in front of her, around her, just like she felt the tight fingers that wrapped around her upper arms and guided her towards the shape of the dark cottage. She heard them, but she didn't understand what they meant. Time was slipping past her like running water through an outstretched hand, the waking world was slipping away, and in its place was a world of shadows and torchlight, of beating hooves, and dancing couples.

The last image she truly registered from her world was the couple being pushed in front of her, James and Kieran, and she thinks they should be grateful. At least they were united in their torment. And then her head dipped below the surface and she was back inside the castle, or the castle as it had been. The woman, her face of shadows, and her dress of starlight was beckoning her to follow down a twisting spiral staircase. So, Alina picked up the heavy skirts she knew she hadn't been wearing and followed.

CHAPTER SIX

Distant voices floated around her, noise scattering like a flurry of snow as she climbed further down into the dark. Her eyes were fixed on the flickering light of the woman's torch and the way her inky hair fell down her shoulders. It was cooler the farther down they went until the woman finally stepped gracefully off the last step and into what looked like an old wine cellar. The floor was earth, and roughly hewn casks lined each stone wall. The woman stared at her with eyes that were both fire bright and ice cold.

"Alina, sit." She said, low and sweet. There was a wrongness in that voice, a familiarity that made her temples ache and gooseflesh break out down her back and arms. "Alina," she said again, but this time there was a warning in her tone. "Sit."

She sank obediently down to the musty earth, tucking her legs underneath her. The white gown she knew she hadn't been billowed around her legs, settling on the cold ground. She traced her finger over the dark, slightly damp dirt, staring down resolutely at her lap. The woman's face still danced with shadows, but Alina didn't want to see whatever was hidden there. She was sure that if she did, she would lose what was left of her sanity.

"Have I lost my mind?" She finally asked softly.

The woman laughed suddenly and with such force that Alina could only sit shocked. She eventually quieted her laughter, her orange eyes shone out of the shadows, suddenly serious as they had just been filled with mirth. "No, you aren't mad. No."

"Who are you? Why do I keep seeing you? Why am I here?" She asked.

A small, terrible smile twisted on the woman's red lips. It was the kind of smile that made nausea boil up in her belly and lodged a scream in the middle of her throat. Above them, music trickled down the staircase, but now that too seemed wrong, out of tune. In another world was the distant wail of voices, a ghost of sensation across her cheek. All at once she came to the awful realization.

"You're me... But you can't be me, I don't-I don't look like you do. I don't live in the same world as you do!" She exclaimed in a voice that was both weak with disbelief and shrill with knowledge.

"You are the us of *now*." The woman explained calmly, seeming almost amused by Alina's distress. "I am the us of *then*."

"What is that supposed to mean?" She pressed. "This isn't real, it can't be real! I'm just having some sort of mental break."

"And what reason do you have for going mad?"

She asked.

The question shocked Alina into a silence. She squeezed her eyes shut when she answered. "Darius. He, he's leaving. He's going into battle, one that I was banned from joining. He just-he *let* them lock me away. Me and our friends. I thought when we fought, we would do it together. He promised we would do it together." She said, feeling the ache in her chest when she relived those last moments when he let them carry her away.

The woman rolled her eyes, her red lips sneering. "Men will do what men always do when they think they are right. This should not be a surprise to you, for a woman of our age. The real question isn't why did he let them carry you away, it's why did *you* let them take you away?"

Alina didn't know what to say.

The woman continued. "We face many choices, in every lifetime, choices that define us. You made a choice when you freed him from that cage, you made another when you smuggled him from your country, and you made the very moment you let them drag you away."

"I want to undo it." Alina said at once. This sudden feeling of regret overwhelming her with the urge to move, to do something. "I've always fought before and I *know* they need me there. I don't know how I know but I do." A rush of tears gathered in her eyes. "But I wasted it, it's too late, I'm locked in this cellar." No sooner had she spoken the words then a thick iron gate slammed shut over the entrance of the stairs.

The woman rose to her feet, a wicked smile stretching across her mouth as she laid one pale hand over the bulky lock. "Then I suppose it's good that we cannot be caged." Liquid fire pulsed through her veins, making them glow an ethereal crimson red. The metal around her palm began to glow, melting under the white-hot heat until the iron was nothing more than a thick dripping ooze puddling on the damp floor. Her orange eyes flicked back to meet hers. "You understand, don't you? What you have to do?"

"I don't understand anything!" She argued. "You haven't explained anything to me and I'm still not sure this is even real... I followed Darius to these people and now he-he let them-"

"Stop!" The woman snarled, all at once venomous and biting. "If you try to tell me what he *let* them do one more time, I will leave you here to rot inside your own mind. Quit following. Lead. You know what it is you must do."

"I don't know how my powers work." Alina told her. A tug behind her naval and the cellar around her wavered like a reflection in still water. "No, no, no, I can't go back yet!" She pleaded. "I don't know how to do what you did; I don't understand why you called me here, I-I still have so many questions. Please don't send me back."

"Too much time has already been wasted and you will need all the time you can get." She said. "No one can cage us, if you remember that then you may make it in time."

"In time for *what*?" She asked desperately. "You have to help me."

"You've forgotten. You can't rely on anyone but yourself. Not when it matters most." The woman said.

Alina's mouth opened, desperately gulping in air as the darkened cellar and torch light whirled around her. For the second time today, she was drowning. An image, unbidden, came to her then, James with the oar, striking Captain Vane. "You're wrong." She gasped and then the woman, the cellar, the castle, it was all gone.

The room stopped spinning so abruptly, she had to dig her fingers into the earth below just to ground herself. When she opened her eyes, James's face, his brow furrowed, lips bitten red, swam into focus. "Whoa, easy there, love. Just breathe. That's it." His hands were anchors, keeping her from sliding down the wall she was propped against. "You had Kieran worried sick." He claimed and Kieran rolled his eyes over his shoulder. "I thought we'd have to drop you round the looney bin after we got out of this fucking basement."

"Cellar." She choked, fingers scrambling for purchase in his jacket, using the leverage to pull herself to her feet. "It's a cellar."

"Same fucking thing." He quipped, raising from his crouch. He watched her warily as she spun in a slow circle. "You all right?" It looked exactly like the cellar in her dream, same earthen floor, same old casks, same iron gate blocking the stairs.

"We have to get out of here. We have to stop them. They're all going to die; they have no idea what they're walking into." She said urgently.

"It's a bit late for that, love." James said.

"Don't be stupid, they aren't leaving until tomorrow night." She argued.

"Right, except that out of the two of us in this conversation, I'm the lucid one, so I actually know what the fuck is going on and-"

"Would you just get to the fucking point?" She snapped.

"Jesus, testy. It is tomorrow, by the way. You were out of it all night, most of today too." He said.

"That's-It's not possible." She said, shaking her head. "It's only been a few hours."

"It's been hours, love." James said softly. "It's too late. Kieran can't touch iron, some Fae shite, and I already tried breaking it down."

She paced in front of the iron gate. Up three, down three, repeat. "I cannot be caged. I cannot be caged." She muttered.

"That's nice... I'm just going to stand over here by my boyfriend. Not that I don't enjoy watching you fall apart in front of me, but if you decide to go all...flamey, I think I'd rather be outside of smiting distance." James said, backpedaling towards his boyfriend.

She came to a stop, glancing quickly at James. "That's it. I know what to do. James, I need you to hit me."

"Hit you?!" He squawked. "I'm not going to hit you."

"I need to feel like I'm in danger, real danger. That's how I found my powers last time. I need you to do this for me." She said earnestly. "I can get us out of here, but I can't do it if you don't help me."

"Love, I can't. I can't hit you." He said. "If you haven't noticed, I'm not a violent person. I *can't*."

"James-"

"I'll do it." Kieran interjected. "I can do it."

"Well that alarmingly didn't take much persuasion." James muttered.

Kieran sighed. "I can feel the moon, it's on the rise, James. We don't have the time to debate this." He walked towards her, squaring his shoulders. "How hard?"

"As hard as you can. I need to feel pain, I need to feel like I'm in danger." She said and took a deep breath, closing her eyes, letting the tension bleed from her body. It would do neither of them any good if she was expecting it.

"Jesus, Kieran, you can't be serious." She heard James say and then pain exploded across the right side of her face. It was the kind of pain that washed the color from the world, made it spin. When her eyes opened again, they were not her own. She could feel the heat pouring through her veins, blooming in the tips of her fingers. Unlike last time, she didn't feel overwhelmed by the sudden power, she felt in control of it.

Her heartbeat was loud and steady in her ears.

She reached out and grasped the iron padlock, curling her fingers tightly around it until the metal pressed indents into her palm. The heat from her fingertips transferred through the warming metal, and just like in her vision, the padlock was glowing, melting until it was nothing more than a molten ooze dribbled onto the earth.

"Okay, that's swell and all but last time you went all fiery you couldn't turn it off. Your clothes were starting to catch on fire, love, and call me crazy, but I don't actually want to see your tits. Do you not remember this? Because that information has been scorched into my brain."

"James," she started, yanking the iron gate off its hinges, throwing it at his feet. "Shut *up*. We have to hurry." She met his eyes, seeing the worry there. She reached out, touching his cheek, feeling his muscles twitch violently under her palm as if expecting a burn. She smiled gently. "I've got it under control." She quickly turned away, jogging up the stairs. "For now." She muttered under her breath.

A figure cut from shadow, stepped in the arch of the doorframe at the top of the stairs, blocking their escape. "I knew there was going to be some sort of escape attempt. I knew you couldn't be trusted. So, what's the rush? Have to run and warn your friends at Titan? Because you're too late. They left an hour ago."

"Brigid?" Kieran asked. "Why aren't you with the others?"

"I just told you." Her pretty face twisted in a sneer. "I expected you three to try something stupid, but I'm surprised with you, Kieran. I guess I thought you cared more about your people than some whore." She was dressed for battle, her auburn hair was pulled back from her face in a tight braid, and a leather harness, studded with the hilts of throwing knives, was strapped over her black tunic. Suddenly, Alina understood, and the heat she collected in her palm evaporated back into her blood.

"Whore? Is she talking about me? Well, that's just fucking rude." James said, jabbing his finger at her. "I'll have you know; I've never once charged for it. Am I a slutty drunk? Yes. Am I easy? Probably. But I have never-"

"Cut the shit, Brigid." Alina interrupted. "You were left behind, same as us, and if you don't shut your mouth and come with us, a lot of people, your people, are going to die." She stared her down, neither one of them blinking until Brigid stepped aside.

"We'll take Kieran's Land Rover, we can cut cross country, it'll be faster." She said and spun around, her braid whipping behind her as she walked quickly towards the cottage door. She yanked the door open. "Well are you coming or not? We don't have time for you three to stand gawking at me from the stairs."

"Jesus," James muttered. "I think I have whiplash."

"Shut up James." She and Kieran spoke together, sharing a small smile as they hurried from the cottage. Outside, the remaining Fae in the camp watched them anxiously as they piled into the Land Rover. Brigid snatched the keys out of Kieran's hands.

"I'm driving, get in." She raised her voice, shouting over the turn of the engine. "The rest of you get back! Clear a path!" She barked and no sooner had she spoken when they were peeling through the camp and up the grassy slope where Alina and Darius had hiked just the day before.

Alina braced her hands on the roof, trying not to smack heads with James as they were jostled in the back. Brigid let out a wild laugh as they crested the top of the hill, and it may have been the most beautiful sound that Alina had ever heard. "Hold on!" She shouted. "It's going to be a bumpy ride, but we might just make it in time. They took the main road, didn't want to be suspicious until they were there." And then they were careening down the slope, and Alina did smack her head against James.

"Ow, fuck." He whined. "This is rougher than that time I tried to have a threesome with those lads from the docks."

Kieran slowly turned around, staring back at him from the front, one brow arched.

"It was years ago! Jesus…"

Alina couldn't help the hysterical peel of laughter that slipped from her mouth on what had to be the strangest night of her life. They were going to make it in time. They were going to save the children; they were just going to do it smartly. They were going to make it in time.

CHAPTER SEVEN

They didn't make it in time.

The Titan Corporation outpost was outside of the city of Cork, nestled in the little community of Spur Hill. Brigid guided the Land Rover back onto a single paved road, turning off the headlights as they passed darkened cottages and farmhouses. They followed the lane up another hill when Brigid slowed almost to a complete stop. On one side, there was an open, white painted gate, its drive leading up to a quaint, two-story family home. On the other side of the lane, there was a crumbling stone wall, nearly overtaken by ivy and wild hedgerows. It opened like a gaping maw of broken teeth to a dirt track running through an unkept field and then dipping down a slope. At the bottom, Alina could see the high walls and sleek, modern design of the Titan outpost. A single red light was blinking slowly, illuminating the field of dead grass in five second intervals.

"There's no police, no sirens, nothing." Alina said. "You'd think the people in those houses we passed would have called it in if they heard gunfire."

"Then you should have looked closer." Brigid said. "There were no lights, not a single car, or barking dog. Titan probably bought up all those houses when they first bought this land. They wouldn't want any scrutiny from the public."

"Oh." Alina said softly.

"Never mind that now. We'll have to leave the rover." Brigid said quietly. "Even with the lights off, they'll see it coming, clear as day." She pointed to the clump of hazel trees, growing feral along the hedgerow. "We'll stick to the trees and keep to their shadows while we go downhill." She pulled the rover into the ditch and Alina cracked her door open. It was nearly silent. Not a sound besides the rustle of wind through the thick, green leaves. She strained to listen, to hear some sound from the others, but there was nothing. A sudden, odd vibrating from one of the trees above made her startle but Brigid was shaking her head.

"Just a bird." She whispered. "My ma used to call them Tairne Lins and hearing one is a mighty bad omen."

"I think we must have beaten them here after all. Surely we'd hear gunfire otherwise." Alina said. "We can just wait here to intercept them."

But Brigid was staring it her with an expression Alina didn't want to look too far into. "No, there's blood in the air, girl, I can smell it and I'd wager that Kieran can smell it too." She paused and Alina saw the gooseflesh rise on the skin of her arms as she surveyed the pulsating light from the outpost. "Something wicked has transpired here. We must look for survivors. That's all we can do now. Quickly, all of you, into the trees." But Alina couldn't move. How could she? There was blood in the air. The man that she loved, the one that left her behind, he could be-

"Wait!" Alina called softly, unwilling to finish that thought. "Give me one of your knives, something with a high melting point."

Brigid eyed her skeptically. "Do you know how to use one without cutting your thumb off?" She asked, but she was already digging through her harness. "Here." She said and offered her the hilt of a smooth, black blade. "It's a tungsten, you won't be able to melt it but they're brittle. It's supposed to be ornamental; you might not be able to use it more than once, so I'd make it count."

"Thank you." Alina said, curling her fingers around the wooden hilt.

"Hey, I think I should be getting one of those." James said, pushing towards them. "I'm not walking into that creepy red Satan light without a weapon. Especially with all that talk of wicked deeds and blood in the air, for fuck's sake woman."

Before Kieran could catch him, Brigid had another knife point to his throat, snarling quietly into his face. "And if you call me anything but my name again, I'll neuter you."

"Well the jokes on you, love because I've never known your name. I don't even think I know her name." He pointed to Alina, winking when Brigid looked away to sheath her knife with a frustrated breath.

"Darlin', you've got to work on your self-preservation." Kieran said and bent down to retrieve a thick hazel branch that must have broken from one of the trees. "Use this, you always say you're good at hitting people in the head with something heavy." James took the offered branch with a roll of his eyes, staying mercifully quiet as they picked their way through the trees and towards the outpost. Well, he stayed quiet for thirty seconds at least.

"But why can't I have a knife?" He whined. They were walking in a pair in front of her. It probably shouldn't have but seeing them interact together made her distinctly more aware of the empty place beside her.

"The last time you used a knife, you needed three stitches." Kieran reminded softly.

"That's completely beside the point, and I was cooking last time." James argued.

"That doesn't add points in your favor." Brigid stopped once they were at the bottom of the hill, they were at the end of their hazel trees. Kieran used the pause to grip the side of James's face, bringing his attention back to him. "Darlin', you need to stay by me, do you understand? No games, you stick to me like glue."

"Yeah, babe," James answered, his voice soft. "You won't be able to shake me off." Their lips slanted together in a tender kiss and Alina had to look away from such an intimate moment. Jealousy, bitter and strong, rose in her throat. That was what love looked like. That should have been them, united together against whatever obstacle they needed to face.

"Oh my God..." Brigid breathed, and the moment was broken, the three of them joined her at the edge of the trees. Alina felt the breath catch in her throat.

At the bottom of the hill, the grass was scorched, Darius must have transformed then, at least while they were outside. The wind shifted, blowing the breeze in their direction, and James turned, retching into the dirt behind them. The air smelled of smoke, dead grass, and charcoaled meat. There were shapes she hadn't noticed before, toppled in the grass. Just smoldering remains shaped like men and women. Some of them were burnt beyond any recognition besides the shining metal of their Titan ID badges. Others were clearly the ones they were here to find, their fair skin and silver hair, glowing ethereally in the light of the full moon, was spattered in blood. The bodies left a crumb trail to the front entrance of the outpost, the heavy, re-enforced door were ripped from its hinges, spilling yellow, artificial light into the night.

"My uncle!" Kieran exclaimed suddenly, as if waking from a dream and grabbed James by the wrist, dragging him forward towards the door.

"Kieran! Kieran, wait!" Brigid called. "They

could have left it open for a trap!" Kieran didn't look back, he and James weaved through the smoldering shapes in the grass, disappearing through the open door. "Curse him!" Brigid spat. She caught Alina's eye. "Stay close, try not to look at the dead or they may try to take you with them." She leapt gracefully through the field of dead silhouettes while Alina walked stiffly in her footsteps, her chin tilted up to resist the temptation of looking down.

Brigid slipped through the open door first, waving her through. Inside, it was somehow worse. Outside, she could ignore the dark, wet patches of earth, the silhouettes with no eyes. But inside, the sterile, white floor was streaking with browning blood, and these dead all had eyes and faces frozen in the throes of death. She felt a soft hand slip inside hers, twisting their fingers together. She lifted her eyes from the dead Titan employee as Brigid squeezed her hand.

"We have to find Kieran and his boy, and I *need* you to help me. I can't do this by myself Alina." She said.

Alina offered her a watery smile. "Even on the ship...I've never-I've never seen-"

"I know, but we have people that are counting on us right now. So, do what you need to do to push it back, there'll be time for tears later." She said and gave her hand another iron squeeze. Alina wiped her eyes, glancing around the building's lobby.

"There's more blood going downstairs then up. I'll bet that's where they headed." She told her.

"Atta girl." Brigid smiled proudly and led the way to the top of the stairs. "You stay behind me and keep an ear out. We don't need anybody sneaking up on us. A fight in a stairwell is something I could live without."

There was no more talk between them was they made their way down into the basement. Through the window in the door, Alina could see James and Kieran kneeling in front of another body on the floor. The two women rushed to their side, Alina's heart in her throat as she prayed it wasn't Darius.

"The king," Brigid whispered, her steps stuttering to a halt.

James had his hand on Kieran's shoulder, steadying his boyfriend as he put pressure on the wound ripped into Midhir's chest. Blood poured in streams between Kieran's fingers, to join the lake of it pooling in the hollow of his uncle's chest. "We just have to get you back to the camp, uncle. Aileen is gifted in the art of healing. I'm going to get you home." Kieran said quickly, so much unlike his usual slow drawl. He twisted his head back to look at them. "Don't just stand there! Help me get him up. Brigid, bring the rover around." He looked at them, his eyes shining with unshed tears. "What are you waiting for? Move!"

"Babe," James began.

"No! Someone help me get him up. I can save him."

"Kieran," Midhir croaked, fresh blood spilling down his chin from his opened mouth. "My boy, I've lost too much blood. I can't move my legs, lad. I know I'm not long left on this world. Time has finally come for me to pass this on." His voice was growing weaker, his words no more than a gargling slur. He lifted a shaky hand, smearing slick blood over the glowing emerald ring of Croí as he pulled it off his finger. He pressed it into Kieran's palm. "I should have listened, now, the people will listen to you."

"Uncle... I couldn't ever replace you." Kieran whispered, tears rolling down his cheeks. "I'm not ready for this. Please let me help you."

"I wouldn't give this to you if I didn't think you were ready for it." He coughed, spraying blood and spittle. "Our people respect tradition. They will listen to their king." The corners of his mouth pulled up into a fond smile. "That's you now." A rattling, wheezing breath left his chest and he was gone. The smile was frozen on his face even as his eyes grew glassy, as lifeless as a doll's. Kieran's hand curled into a fist over the ring as sobs wracked his body. James rubbed his hand soothingly up and down his back as he wept over his uncle's still corpse. Brigid was standing as rigid as a statue at her side, silent tears sliding down her cheeks.

After a moment to offer comfort, James rose to his feet, walking towards them. He wiped his own tears away with the back of his hand. "He was talking more before you two got here." He cleared his throat. "A few of the Fae got away, they ran before they even got into the building. That's why we didn't see their car."

"Cowards." Brigid spat.

"Yeah, well, you were wrong about one thing, Lina." He told them. "They weren't expecting an attack. From the way the old man told it, they about shit themselves when Darius came swooping out of the sky with his fire. It's how the few of them made it this far in."

"Where is he?"

"Where are the children?" She and Brigid asked at once.

"Gone. They're all gone, Lina. Drugged him with a massive sedative when he turned back to come in and save the kids. The king and the couple guys he had left tried to stop them, but it wasn't enough. He said he watched them pack up and leave, took a copter from the roof is what he said it sounded like."

"That's why this place is so empty." Brigid muttered.

"Did he know where they were taking them? Did he hear what they said?" Alina asked frantically.

"They're going after the rest of the shifters." Kieran had pushed himself to his feet, he slid the ring onto his finger. "The last of the dragon shifters. They're in hiding, in Norway. That's where they're going, and they took the kids and

Darius with them."

"That actually makes sense." Alina said slowly. "Titan's main headquarters is in Oslo. They won't hurt them. They're just consolidating. They probably want their subjects in the same lab after the stunt I pulled in New York." She took a step away from them and then another. "I'm going. I have to go after him. I promised him that I would never let them experiment on him and I meant it."

Kieran held up his hand. "Alina, wait."

"I don't have time; I have to find him!" She argued.

"You don't have any money, you're wanted by the police, and you have no way to get off this island." Kieran said firmly. "Let me bury my uncle, and I can help you. They have my people too." His hands were covered in the drying blood of the last family he had in this world. Maybe it was the sight of that blood, dripping from the tips of his fingers onto the basement floor that had her nodding. After all, they all had stake in this fight.

CHAPTER EIGHT

The drive back to the Fae camp was a lot more solemn then the ride there. All four of them were squished into the front of the rover, no one wanted to share the back with the dead. It was daybreak when they finally arrived back, the camp had received its own version of the news from the defectors if the cries drifting out of tents like the remnants of a bad dream, were anything to go by. Kieran was out of the rover first, his fist cracking across the jaw of one of the men Alina recognized from the gathering they had around the fire.

"Coward!" He roared, his fingers curling into fists at his sides. "If I weren't wearing this ring, I swear I'd beat you to death."

"He made *you* king?" He said, spitting a wad of blood into the dirt as he pushed himself to his feet. Their dramatic return had caught the attention of the others who were gathering around their group. The people began to talk amongst themselves once they saw what Alina had seen from the first time she had ever seen Kieran, a strong man, a good man, a leader. The only difference was the emerald ring that rested on his middle finger of his right hand.

"He did. After you and the others left your king to die." Kieran asserted. A hush fell over the crowd around them, broken only by a single muffled sob.

"We had to leave! We thought they were already dead, Kieran, and we would have ended up dead with them."

"Well he wasn't dead. And if you had bothered to stay by his side like you were sworn to, maybe you could have brought him back here to be healed. Remind me, what does our law say is to happen to those that commit treason?" He asked casually.

"You can't be serious, Kieran-My King, you don't mean to kill us."

"No, no one else should lose their lives today. I want you and whatever men deserted with you to collect your families from the camp and leave. I don't want to see you again. You have no protection, no aid, no contact from the others. From today on, you're on your own." Kieran said.

"But-"

"And if you're not gone within the next hour, then your family can watch your execution instead. Now tell me that you understand what I'm saying to you." He demanded.

"Yes." He bit out and shoved through the crowd to grab his belongings.

James whistled. "Jesus, babe, that was a bit much, don't you think?"

"No, actually, my uncle is dead and if they had waited, maybe they could have gotten him out." Kieran said. "The rest of you, build a funeral pyre, prepare the dead." He didn't wait to see that his orders were followed, just walked into his uncle's cottage, and slammed the door.

"Don't just stand there!" Brigid snapped. "You heard the king, start getting wood. I need people here to move the bodies." She instructed as she took charge of the arrangements.

Alina caught James by the crook of his arm as he tried to follow Kieran inside. "Give him a few minutes." She said softly. "You have to give him time to process his loss."

James scraped a hand through his hair, smearing dirt and dried blood through his blond locks. "I can't just sit around doing fuck all."

"I know, believe me, I know. There's been a lot of death, and a lot of failure. But I'm sure Brigid will have something to keep us busy." She said and squeezed his arm.

Despite not getting any sleep the night before, they worked through the morning and afternoon with the other Fae to make funeral pyres for the fallen. She didn't mind the work, not even after the fourth splinter she got in her palm. It kept her mind off Darius, off Titan, and what they would be doing with the love of her life. Failure was never easy; each broken promise was another weight laid over her back.

Kieran didn't come out until the pyres were

built and the bodies moved, not even to watch the deserters and their procession from the camp. They gathered in silence, waiting for someone to start speaking. Kieran finally cleared his throat.

"Alina, would you light the pyres?" He asked quietly.

"Of course." She said and looked around for a torch or lighter. It took her a second to realize what exactly he was asking her to do. She walked to each one, laying her hand on the branches they collected, and willed them to alite. When she had finished, she took her place beside Kieran and James and observed as he watched his uncle burn. No one left until there was nothing but smoldering ash and kindling, glowing red and orange in the moonless night. When it was just the four of them, Kieran spoke again.

"Brigid, I want you to start talking to the people. I want volunteers to go through combat training, anyone that agrees to go will be coming with us to Norway. I need as big an army as I can get."

"If you asked them yourself, each and every one would go. They'll follow if you ask them to." She said and then looked carefully at Alina. "But going to Oslo...It'll be the ruin of our people. Those children are gone, Kieran, beyond saving, and we got what we wanted. Titan left Ireland; their outpost is abandoned now."

"She's right." Alina said suddenly. "You've done more than enough for Darius and me. I'll go to

Oslo, and I'll free him. And if the children are there, I'll make sure they get home. I can't ask anyone to risk their lives for us, I just can't. You should stay here and help your people rebuild."

"It won't matter if they go back to their lives, if they have more children, Titan will come back. They don't just have Darius, uncle said they were going after the last of the dragon shifters. They've been underground for hundreds of years, but they must have some way to track them now. Don't you get it?" He asked incredulously. "If they can do that then what's stopping them from coming back and getting the rest of us? Or going after the Selkies next? If someone doesn't stop them now, then what's to stop them from systematically harvesting every supernatural person and creature on this earth?" He looked away, staring back into the embers. "I won't force anyone to go, it will be a volunteer basis only. Our people have been hiding, withering away for years, if this is our extinction event, then I want to go out and meet it head on, I'm done hiding."

Brigid finally broke the silence that fell over them. "I suppose a warrior's death is the most honorable." She laid her hand over his shoulder, squeezing softly. "I'll speak with them if you want me to, but I think they would take it better if they heard it from their king."

He finally nodded. "Tomorrow. Today has been two days too long. James," he took his boyfriends hand. "Let's go to bed."

"Yeah, gimme a second." He offered Alina a tired smile. "We'll get him back. You two are so in love it's annoying." He snagged her hand, another link in their chain. "Come get some rest. I have a feeling we won't be getting much of that for a while."

"Yeah, thanks." She said and let him drag her towards the cottage. James and Kieran were asleep almost as soon as their heads hit the pillow, but as she lay beside them in the bed that was too narrow for three grown adults, she ignored the ache in her heart and watched the mist roll in over the green hills through the window as she waited for sleep to claim her.

End

THE DRAGON'S RETURN

Book 3 in the Chaos and Flames Series
By Evelyn Winters

> "For last year's words belong
> to last year's language
> And next year's words await another voice.
> And to make an end is to make a beginning."
> ~T.S. Eliot

CHAPTER 1

Despite not getting any sleep the night before, they worked through the morning and afternoon with the other Fae to make funeral pyres for the fallen. She didn't mind the work, not even after the fourth splinter she got in her palm. It kept her mind off Darius, off Titan, and what they would be doing with the love of her life. Failure was never easy; each broken promise was another weight laid over her back.

Kieran didn't come out until the pyres were built and the bodies moved, not even to watch the deserters and their procession from the camp. They gathered in silence, waiting for someone to start speaking. Kieran finally cleared his throat.

"Alina, would you light the pyres?" He asked quietly.

"Of course." She said and looked around for a torch or lighter. It took her a second to realize what exactly he was asking her to do. She walked to each one, laying her hand on the branches they collected, and willed them to alite. When she had finished, she took her place beside Kieran and James and observed as he watched his uncle burn. No one left until there was nothing but smoldering ash and kindling, glowing red

and orange in the moonless night. When it was just the four of them, Kieran spoke again.

"*Brigid, I want you to start talking to the people. I want volunteers to go through combat training, anyone that agrees to go will be coming with us to Norway. I need as big an army as I can get.*"

"*If you asked them yourself, each and every one would go. They'll follow if you ask them to.*" *She said and then looked carefully at Alina.* "*But going to Oslo...It'll be the ruin of our people. Those children are gone, Kieran, beyond saving, and we got what we wanted. Titan left Ireland; their outpost is abandoned now.*"

"*She's right.*" *Alina said suddenly.* "*You've done more than enough for Darius and me. I'll go to Oslo, and I'll free him. And if the children are there, I'll make sure they get home. I can't ask anyone to risk their lives for us, I just can't. You should stay here and help your people rebuild.*"

"*It won't matter if they go back to their lives, if they have more children, Titan will come back. They don't just have Darius, uncle said they were going after the last of the dragon shifters. They've been underground for hundreds of years, but they must have some way to track them now. Don't you get it?*" *He asked incredulously.* "*If they can do that then what's stopping them from coming back and getting the rest of us? Or going after the Selkies next? If someone doesn't stop them now, then what's to stop them from systematically harvesting every supernatural person and creature on this earth?*" *He looked away, staring back into the embers. "I won't force anyone to go, it will be a volunteer basis only. Our people have been hiding, withering away for years, if this is our extinction event, then I want to go out and meet it head on, I'm done hiding."*

Despite his passionate words after his uncle's funeral, Kieran was the one that forced Alina to wait. She wanted to leave the second she woke up the next morning, the uncertainty about her lover's fate was almost too much for her to bare. She even threatened to go after Titan by herself after he said they needed time to prepare, but Kieran did eventually get through to her. Running into a confrontation blind and unprepared was what got them into this situation in the first place, and Titan wasn't going to kill Darius or the Fae children, they wanted to use them like lab rats. It had been a week since then and Alina was still training. This time, she wouldn't be left behind or caught unawares. This time, she would break free.

Light danced across the tents set up in the middle of the white stone ring, throwing shadows across the fairy camp. The sun was high in the early morning sky, the almost constant cover of clouds thin enough to let the white-hot heat penetrate the Fae camp. The few people that remained were hanging their laundry while the others practiced. There was no shortage of chores but there was also very little time to prepare for the coming fight.

Alina was panting, chest heaving, lungs burning

for air kind of panting. Back in the city she had Pilates three days a week with a personal trainer, that was nothing compared to Kieran's training. Every night she ached, muscles she didn't even know she had throbbed every time she lay down to sleep and every morning she felt much better until she actually moved to crawl out of bed and fresh aches had her hobbling all the way to the shower.

She wiped a thin sheen of sweat off her brow and once more raised the sword out in front of her, though her arms were screaming for a break, it should feel like an extension of her arm Kieran had explained. Her opponent was James, his bottle-blond hair was damp and hanging limply around his face, his pale skin dewy with perspiration. His pale, grey-blue eyes sparkled in amusement as he circled her. His footwork was perfect, as usual, and she did her best to mirror his fluid movements. James had taken to their training like a fish to water much to Alina's constant aggravation.

He moved like he was dancing, one step to the side, a flick of his slender wrist and her sword flew from her hand, clattering down onto one of the smooth, white fairy stones. He had her disarmed, again. A scream of frustration was building in her throat and most likely showed on her face if the way James danced back was any indication. He tossed his own sword down and raised his hands in surrender.

"Don't turn those Satan eyes on me, love, I can't

help being naturally talented," he said quickly, but that only seemed to fan the flame of her anger.

"I just don't understand why I'm so clumsy with a sword!" She exclaimed in frustration, lowering herself to the ground for a much-needed break.

"Uh...Maybe because you're just clumsy in general?" James suggested unhelpfully. "You're the only person I've ever seen that can trip over thin air and you can't even walk in a straight line! I'd forgive you if you were a lush but no," he shook his head slowly, "you're painfully, painfully sober and that just makes it more pathetic."

"Gee, thanks for the boost of confidence," she said sarcastically.

"That's what I'm here for," he quipped. "It's one of my duties as your best friend."

"You're not my best-friend," she said. "I already have one of those."

"Please tell me you aren't talking about that bird who sent you off on that rotten ship with her creepy fucking father and hasn't bothered to try to contact you since, not that one, please babe," he begged.

She remained stubbornly silent. It really did sound bad when James laid it all out like that.

"You've got to be fucking kidding me, you know that bitch did it on purpose, right?" He pressed her.

"She didn't-she wouldn't-" Alina tried to defend her, but the words didn't come. Maybe Alicia didn't do it on purpose, but it still hurt that she put her on that boat. How could she not know her father was working with Titan? *Maybe she did know*, a treacherous little part of her whispered.

"Ah, come on, fuck her. She was probably one of those little wannabe clingers on anyway. You're better off, babe, even if you reject my generous and humble offer," he said.

"And I'm pretty sure that generous and humble are two things that you have never been described as in your life," she quipped back.

A long shadow fell over them, a quiet, hulking shape blocking the sun. James smiled easily and leaned back on his elbows, his shirt dipped down, exposing more pale skin and sharp collar bones. *Must be Kieran then*, he was the only one James ever cared about impressing.

"Hey babe, come to entertain us or scold us?" James asked.

Kieran looked between the two of them, both slumped into the grass. He didn't look impressed.

"Care to explain why you're not training?" Kieran asked instead.

"But we were! Quite vigorously and then, now this is just me, I don't know 'bout Lins over here, but you see, I suddenly realized it was pointless."

"Thin ice…" Alina tried to warn under her breath, but James wasn't getting the hint.

"Seriously, babe, why are bothering with all this useless shite when Titan is going to take one look at us with our little swords and just shoot us," he continued. "We should be training with *guns*, not swords. We will literally be bringing a knife to a gunfight."

"Guns are loud," Kieran said simply, "and you two need more practice." He walked away from them and back towards the center of the fairy camp.

James groaned, "I still think he's an idiot, we need real weapons if we're going to break into Titan's main headquarters."

Alina shook her head softly in disagreement, "he wants a total and complete stealth operation this time and I agree with him. That's what I wanted to do last time, and no one listened to me."

James shrugged, "sticks and stones, babe. You don't have to say it to me, I was one of the only two that agreed with you last time."

He pushed himself up with a groan, offering a hand to pull her up, "up you get, we better get back to it before Kieran has to come back 'round and administer spankings."

"You'd like that too much for it to be a punishment," she said and quickly jumped back as his practice sword was suddenly thrust at her. Laughter bubbled from her lips, tinkling and high like bells chiming in the warm morning air.

"It's true!" She cried and twisted her body away from another jab of his sword. The banter between them didn't last long the more heated their faux battle became. Alina was panting again, open mouthed, chest heaving for air, but she thought she might have James this time. So far, she'd never been able to disarm him.

Their bodies twisted and lunged side to side, each one trying to get the upper hand on the other, blunted practice swords gleaming in the bright morning sun. James flipped his sword up into the air and caught it with the opposite hand, using the distraction to slap the hand that held the hilt of her practice sword. It clattered to the white stone for probably at least the 9th time that morning and she sighed, slumping into the downy grass one more time.

"I give up," she groaned. "You're right, it is pointless and I'm terrible at it."

"You aren't really used to losing, are you babe?" James asked and sat gingerly beside her.

"No, not really, not until recently," she answered softly.

"Shite, sorry… Probably shouldn't have mentioned anything, but you know me, no filter, babe," he rambled.

"No, it's okay. I'm just struggling because the last time we were together, Darius and I, he was leaving me."

"He wasn't leaving you, leaving you though," James said.

"No, but he was still leaving. He didn't trust me and that's what hurts the most. I still think about it, almost every day… And then, there's-"

"The woman will not be going either." He said and Alina glanced at Brigid, unable to believe that such a

skilled warrior wouldn't be joining the king and his men, only to find her staring straight back at her. Oh…

"Darius and I go together. I know how badly you need him to help you. I'm not trying to be rude, but you know that you need him if you're going to have even a chance." She hissed. Helping the Fae recover their children had been her idea, she wasn't about to let them sideline her. "If I don't go, then Darius doesn't."

"Lina…" Darius began gently, but she turned to him before he could finish, catching the guilt in his expression.

It was as if a pit had opened been opened beneath her feet. She was falling, she had to be falling. "Darius, you can't be serious. We decided this together. You said we'd do this together." She pleaded. "What happened to restoring our honor? Or whatever the hell it was you said?"

"In completing this quest, I will restore honor to both of our names, but I must do this. Not only for you but for my people. This could repair our relationship with the Fae. An ally would not be something to take for granted in this age."

"I can't-I don't understand." And she didn't. She was still falling, now accompanied by roaring in her ears and a black shroud slowly cloaking her sight.

"I am sorry, my Lina, this is far too dangerous of a pursuit for you anyway." He said and she was vaguely aware of his lips pressing against the overheated skin on her forehead.

"Darius…" She pleaded one last time.

"I will regale you with tales of my victory upon my

return." He promised, but how could he not see that she was falling?

"Take them to the cellar room." She heard Midhir say. "I want them secure while we plan our attack. They are not to be allowed to run loose among my people until our return."

"Yes, Tiarna."

"Wait, wait just a minute, cellar room? Are you locking us up? I am not going in some fucking cellar. Kieran!"

"Uncle, you can't possibly think that imprisoning them for two days is a fair treatment of our guests."

"Then you can join them!"

"Uncle!"

She heard this taking place, beyond her, in front of her, around her, just like she felt the tight fingers that wrapped around her upper arms and guided her towards the shape of the dark cottage. She heard them, but she didn't understand what they meant. Time was slipping past her like running water through an outstretched hand, the waking world was slipping away, and in its place was a world of shadows and torchlight, of beating hooves, and dancing couples.

The last image she truly registered from her world was the couple being pushed in front of her, James and Kieran, and she thinks they should be grateful. At least they were united in their torment. And then her head dipped below the surface and she was back inside the castle, or the castle as it had been. The woman, her face made of shadows, and her dress of starlight, was beckoning her to follow down a twisting spiral stair-

case. So, Alina picked up the heavy skirts she knew she hadn't been wearing and followed.

"Lina?" James interrupted the sudden memory and she stared guiltily at her grass stained knees.

"I never told you everything about that night," she finally admitted.

"What are you talking about? The night of the raid? In case you've forgotten, I was there. I was there for the whole bloody, horrible mess," he said.

"Not for all of it," she contradicted. "You weren't there when I went away."

"Went away? You mean your mad little comatose episode? Yeah, Kieran and I already agreed to never mention that again, so you don't have to-"

"No! You don't understand what you're talking about," she said firmly. "There was-is a woman that I see. Sometimes she comes in my dreams, but other times she comes when I'm awake."

"Yeah, I don't know if I'm the right person for this, you need some medical attention maybe, you know, a professional," he said slowly.

"Would you stop trying to make everything into a joke?! I'm trying to explain something to you, James. I haven't-I haven't told anyone else," she confessed.

"Sorry, I'm listening, babe," he said softly and true to his word, he stayed silent.

"So, there's this woman except, she's me, from hundreds of years ago, but she's still me. She was the one that helped me learn to control my powers down in that cellar. At first, she was great, she helped me, she guided me to do what I needed to do, but now...she's like a poison I can't purge. She tells me that we're better alone, that we're meant to be alone. She wants me to leave, without you, without Kieran, and go to Romania. That's where she says my ancestors were born and that I'm needed there again."

James listened to the whole thing, his brows furrowed, lips set in a pensive frown. He didn't say anything for a long time and then shrugged his shoulders up. "The way I see it, she's dead and you're not. What's she going to do if you don't listen? It's your life now, Lina, not hers, you can do what you want with it."

"When did you get so smart?" She asked, genuinely surprised after how much better she felt after listening to his advice. James was right. It was her life and she made her own choices.

"I've always been smart, I just hide it, really, really well," he winked and slapped her thigh. "Lets' go inside and make Kieran make us breakfast."

"You know he's the king of the Fae," she pointed out and pushed herself to her feet.

"So? He'd be a pretty shitty king if he didn't feed his people," he said and grabbed her hand, tugging her towards the quaint, white cottage that she currently called home. There were moments when she thought of Darius and felt a terror so strong, she thought it would bring her to her knees. She could never forget that, despite the reassurances, she didn't know if he was alive or dead, but there were moments that made it a little easier to bear. She felt the hot sun on her back, the comforting weight of James hand in her own, and catalogued the memory away for a rainy day.

CHAPTER 2

Surprisingly, Kieran only took one look at them shirking their training early to come and beg for food, and wordlessly pulled a carton of eggs from the fridge. James and Alina fist-bumped each other in victory, Kieran did make the best eggs after all. She sat down at the rickety kitchen table and let James go off to flirt. It used to make her embarrassed to watch them, but seeing as James was insatiable and annoying, she had gotten overexposed and now the PDA no longer seemed to phase her.

Whenever Alicia had a boyfriend it was like she ceased to existent. It had happened every time, just like clockwork, Alicia was suddenly too busy to make their lunch dates or go club hopping or to even answer her texts, but it wasn't like that with James. She noticed it immediately, even though their lives seemed to revolve around each other there was room for her there too.

James had his chin hooked over Kieran's shoulder, perched there like a vulture while he cooked. Those beautiful grey eyes were following his every move, but like he felt her watching, he peered back, the corners of his mouth curling in a pleasant smile.

"You okay, babe?" He asked.

"Yeah, yeah, I'm fine," she answered and got up to hip check him, resting comfortably against Kieran's other side. "I want cheese on my eggs, lots and lots of cheese," she demanded.

James wrinkled his nose cutely, "that is absolutely disgusting. No cheese on mine and none of that green healthy shite that you put in there last time."

"You mean spinach?" Kieran asked deadpan.

"Yeah, none of that nasty shite," he said and shuddered.

"I swear it's easier to get a five-year-old to eat their vegetables than you," Kieran huffed softly but the expression on his face was soft and fond.

She hovered next to James as Kieran cooked their eggs and tried to imagine doing something so domestic with Darius. She was worried she wouldn't be able to, their relationship started out so fast and was primarily physical, but she could see it. She would love to watch Darius cook her his favorite meals and then she could return the favor. There was still so much they didn't know about each other. They weren't like James and Kieran who had a history, they were still building theirs, brick by brick, layer by layer, until one day maybe they would be as comfortable with each other as the couple standing next to her.

Kieran served up their eggs and true to his word,

there was extra cheese on Alina's and no spinach in the dish he gave to James. They sat around the rickety table to eat and if Alina caught the two, fully grown men playing footsie under the table, she didn't mention it. James was stuffing more into his mouth than he could reasonably chew, cheeks puffing out like a chipmunk. Kieran grabbed the hand that was currently using the fork as a shovel and stopped James's continuous flow of food.

"If you don't slow down and chew your food, you're going to choke, and I just can't have that, lover," he said softly, the Irish brogue thicker when his voice was low.

"But I'm hungry," James protested around a mouthful of eggs.

"No one's going to take your plate away. I think you'll survive if you eat a little slower," Kieran said and let go of his wrist.

"Bossy, I can't quite tell if I like it or I hate it," James mused but returned to his food at a much slower pace.

"You love it," Kieran said for him and was rewarded by a blob of egg that hit him squarely between the eyes.

"Hah!" James snorted. "I can't believe I actually made that shot!"

"You're an idiot," Kieran deadpanned.

"Ah, but an idiot with skill," James teased, his voice light and airy.

"If both of you don't shut up and finish your

eggs, I'm going to start swiping off your plates," Alina warned. That got them moving at least and both boys shoveled eggs into their mouths, Kieran's lecture already lost even on himself.

They finished breakfast, fought over who had to do the dishes, and just when Kieran was about to force them outside for more practice, they were saved. Dark clouds rolled in from the east and with it brought a chilling rain and low hanging mist. It was so thick it almost looked like a low raising wall, dense and solid against the usual rolling green landscape.

They spent the rest of the late morning and afternoon going over Kieran's plan. It sounded simple, it sounded easy, but most importantly, it sounded like it would work. Alina couldn't help the doubt that poisoned her mind and leeched her confidence, everything always seemed easy until you had to go through with it.

"We'll wait for a public holiday," Kieran reiterated, "if what Alina said is true then they'll have the bare minimum staff on hand."

Alina nodded her head in agreement, "they may be a major corporation, but they still hate to give holiday pay. The building will be run by a skeleton crew, you can trust me on that." She felt somewhat guilty as she said this, it was always one of her first moves in business to find ways to halt raises or get out of paying for holidays and overtime. She hadn't realized how out of touch she had become, not until recently, she had to admit to herself she never really used to think about the employees as being humans themselves, they had become numbers on a spreadsheet to her.

"It adds in our favor that we didn't retaliate against them right away," Kieran continued, "the time between raids might lull them into a false sense of security. They might even think we've given up now that we've lost our biggest weapon."

"Well, our biggest weapon according to them," James said with a sly wink in Alina's direction.

"Aw, that's really sweet, James," Alina said, genuinely touched.

"What? Oh, sorry babe, you thought I meant you? Nah, I was talking about me. I am exceptional with a sword," a lascivious wink aimed at Kieran this time, "and with hitting people about the head with heavy objects."

Kieran gave a long-suffering sigh, one of the sighs that Alina was sure was a long-standing part of their relationship and continued outlining his plan. "We take everyone we have left. We don't have large enough numbers to immediately be detected if Brigid can disable the security system first."

"Large enough numbers? You can say that again, babe. Titan won't be the only ones running with a skeleton crew," James said, and he wasn't wrong. Despite Brigid's confidence at the funeral that the last of the remaining Fae would stand with their new king, many of them had left the camp, and out of those that were still here, only four had volunteered to go to Oslo. Brigid had been furious, but Kieran surprised everyone by letting them go with a promise that they could return to the safe house whenever they needed to. He told them after they had packed up their caravans and left that he hadn't blamed them. There had already been enough lives lost and he wouldn't hold it against them if they valued their own.

"It works in our favor," Kieran insisted, "we don't need a big group bumbling around in the dark."

"Speaking of dark, we should get to bed, especially if Kieran's going to insist on waking us up at the arse crack of dawn again," James said and he was right, somehow the rest of the day had melted away while they had been talking.

"Yeah, sorry," Kieran said and got up to throw their lunch plates into the sink. He shrugged at them, "I'll wash them tomorrow." He said.

Alina pushed herself to her feet while her aching muscles protested and kissed both her boy's goodnight. She stopped at the foot of the stairs, looking back at them pitifully over her shoulder. "Does anyone want to carry me up? I don't think my thighs can actually hold me."

James scoffed and made a flying leap at his boyfriend. It was by repetition and practice that Kieran actually caught him.

"Are you kidding, babe? Kieran's already got to carry me up," James said, dangling from the other man's arms.

She sighed in resignation, "of course he is..." She let Kieran go up first and then somehow managed to drag herself up the stairs and into to her bedroom. Whenever the guest room had stopped being the guest room and instead became her room, she didn't know, but she was comfortable in it and it had started to feel like home. Undressing felt like some sort of torture, so she didn't bother to try and make her muscles move enough to put on her pajamas, she just fell straight into bed and nestled under her copious amounts of covers. It was colder at night without Darius beside her. It was one of those nights that not long after her exhausted body hit the mattress, one second she was awake, and the next she was not.

There was something in the air that night that chilled her cozy cottage room, something that perfumed the air with the smell of damp earth and acrid smoke. She heard the music playing in her dreams, the string instruments and their mournful cry, the steady, triumphant beat of the drums, and the rhythmic clacking of pieces of bone. She had heard it before, but only in one place. The away place, the place she went whenever she saw the woman.

She could feel the suction, like being in a tub after the plugs been pulled, and tried to swim away from it. But moving in a dream was worse than moving through sand and the shadows overcame her, dragging her down to that away place.

Torchlight flickered across the roughhewn

stone walls, casting shadows that danced around the little alcove she found herself in. She immediately saw the woman, her hair in fine, gleaming waves down her shoulders and back, face shrouded in darkness, eyes like liquid flame, piercing the dimness around them.

"What do you want?" Alina demanded, in the last few weeks she had grown accustomed to the woman's games of cat and mouse, but ultimately, a visit meant one thing: she wanted Alina to do something. Lately it was abandoning Darius and her friends to journey to Romania but Alina had firmly refused. Like James said, it was her life now.

"I would expect a little gratitude, this is a courtesy call after all," the woman purred.

"Just tell me whatever it is you have to tell me, no more games," she said firmly.

"No more games," the woman echoed, sounding strangely delighted by the prospect. "You are growing up, aren't you?"

"I'm a grown woman already. If you don't tell me what you have to tell me I'm going to leave," she said, but it was an empty threat and the woman knew it. Alina had no idea how to leave the dreamscape, while the woman had her here, she was stuck, like a fly caught in a web.

"This is a game, whether you want to see it or not, and right now you're losing," the woman told her.

"What do you mean I'm losing?" Alina demanded.

"Plays have been made, pieces on the board moved that cannot be unmoved," she said.

"Just speak plainly!" She shouted which seemed to be the wrong thing to do if the woman's narrowed eyes and sudden icy demeanor were any indication.

"Tomorrow brings with it death, the other half a soul will darken forever," she warned.

"The other half of a soul?" Alina questioned aloud. "Are you talking about a soulmate? Oh my God... Is something going to happen to Darius?"

"I thought you didn't want to play the game?" The woman asked snidely and there was a familiar tugging behind her navel, the plug was about to be pulled again.

"No! You can't send me back yet! Not until you tell me what's going to happen to Darius!"

One second she was asleep and the next, Alina was screaming in her bed, sat upright, eyes wide open, flame already gathered in her hand.

"No! Damn you! You bitch, you fucking bitch!" She raged.

The door to her bedroom exploded inward, Kieran's foot stuck through the center of it, hopping on one leg as he tried to regain his balance. James shoved past his boyfriend and hurried into her little cottage room, stopping immediately to slap a hand over his eyes.

"Jesus Christ, babe, you're tits are out. Put those away before you blind someone," he said.

She pulled the sheet over herself, *I guess I did just*

get undressed and crawl into bed last night, didn't I? She pulled her knees to her chest as her two boys watched her with twin furrows in their brow and a worried pull at their lips. A glance out the window confirmed the sun was just beginning to rise over the horizon, it was a red dawn.

"Alina, are you okay? We could hear you screaming from our room," Kieran told her.

"I-" she stopped herself. She was going to tell them that she was all right, but was she?

"Yeah, you were raving like a right lunatic, not to mention the whole flamey thing you had going on there," James added unhelpfully.

"I'm not okay," she told them truthfully. "Darius is going to die today if we don't get to him."

"Wait, how do you-"

"How the hell are we supposed to get to Oslo on short notice?" They talked over her.

"I don't know, I don't know! But we have to try… I could never forgive myself if I knew what was going to happen and did nothing. We have to get to him, we have to," she said, her voice had broken towards the end, she hated to sound so weak.

"It was probably just a nightmare, you need sometime to calm down," Kieran said but she shook her head resolutely.

"I had another dream, one-one about *her*," she said, glancing meaningfully at James. He nodded his head in understanding, flashing her a thumbs up.

"About her? What are you talking about?"

Kieran asked. James leaned down and affectionately bit softly on his shoulder, Kieran's reaction was instinctual, burying his fingers in James's tousled blond locks and scratching his scalp until the other man was purring like a feline.

"Mm, that's nice… If Lina says Darius is going to die today then he is. You just have to trust her, babe," James said. Kieran nodded slowly.

"Okay, but only because I trust you," he answered softly, "that doesn't mean I don't want an explanation later when we have more time."

James mock saluted to him, "aye aye, captain."

Kieran smiled at him fondly, "you are an idiot." He slapped James on the hip. "Get ready, we have to leave in ten minutes if we want even a chance to get to Oslo before nightfall."

Alina scrambled off her bed, nearly falling face first in the tangle of sheets and blankets that somehow wrapped around her ankles, and hastily threw on whatever clothes were clean and closest. Kieran and James were out through the remains of her shattered door as soon as the sheet went down and she could hear them arguing softly with each other in the room next door.

She made it downstairs first, tapping one boot clad foot impatiently as she waited for her boys by the door. They came down the stairs like they did every morning, with James draped casually over one of Kieran's broad shoulders, long legs dangling nearly to each carpeted step.

"Jesus woman, I can hear the sassy boot tap

from all the way over here. We're coming," James assured her, but she wasn't in the mood for him this morning, not when Darius's life was at stake.

"Just get your shoes on and get out there. I'm going to find Brigid and tell her that the plans changed," she said.

Walking out that door and into the damp, cool morning air wasn't as bracing as it normally was. She was filled with nervous energy that was making her jittery as she walked through the fairy camp. It was quiet, was it always this quiet?

Brigid's tent was the last one, closest to the perimeter of white fairy stone. The sun was still a half risen flame in the east, all the tents dark and silent, save for Brigid. A single flickering flame was lighting the inside of the tent and before Alina could open the flap, Brigid was there. Her red hair cascading freely around her shoulders, instead of her customary braid, she must have caught the other still getting ready for the day.

"Plans have changed," Alina blurted immediately. "We're going to Oslo now and I mean right now so finish getting ready and grab the rest of the volunteers and before you say anything there isn't enough time to talk. I'll explain everything once we're on the way."

"Shut your fucking mouth," Brigid hissed and out of all the possible responses Alina visualized in her head, this was by far the least expected. She opened her mouth to retort but Brigid immediately slapped her palm across her lips, silencing whatever she was about to say. She raised her finger to her lips, shushing her and they both strained to listen.

It sounded like a beast. A roar that was growing steadily louder, faster and faster, as whatever was making that noise hastened their approach. In her peripheral vision she could see James and Kieran stop walking towards them as they too caught onto the noise. Four pairs of eyes slid to the horizon as two monstrous black SUV's careened over the top of the hill, tearing down the little country road towards their camp. There was silver lettering stamped on the side: TITAN Corp.

"Everybody get down!" Brigid roared but it was too late. A hail of gunfire erupted from the open windows of the SUV's and Alina's world was suddenly reduced to a game of survival. Bullets tore up the wet earth in front of her toes, pounding into the mud as she danced back. She felt something hot tear through her right shoulder, but her body didn't give her the time to experience the pain, it was too busy throwing her backwards and out of the way of the next spray.

Tents were shredded, some of the Fae came flying out of the ruined strips of canvas, shrieking as they ran for the house or the fields, some tents stayed ominously quiet. What seemed to stretch on forever was over in just a few seconds as they stopped to reload and in those few seconds of stillness, their lives were changed forever.

CHAPTER 3

Blood splatter. An entire mist of it painted their faces, their arms, their reaching hands with red. The machine gun had torn bullets through his torso in a jagged, gruesome zigzag. His body fell backwards around the same time theirs were diving forward, three pairs of hands tried to catch him. Alina and James fell onto their bellies on the soft mud. James scrambled up to all fours, crawling the rest of the way to his lover. His hands were shaking as they rose to cup Kieran's slack face.

"No, no, no, no, please, lover no." He spoke the words in a quiet rush, tripping over his own tongue.

Brigid hadn't fallen with them and she threw herself forward with cry of rage, her hands dipped into her belt, knifes flew from her fingers and judging by the wet thuds, they met their marks. But Alina didn't watch to see if Brigid got her target or not, her fingers dug into the damp earth as she willed herself the strength to rise. She crawled the last few feet to Kieran's body and methodically began applying pressure to the bullet spray leaking the most blood. His chest was torn apart, but somehow, still rose and fell with breath.

"You have to help me, James," she said urgently. "He's not dead yet but he will be if we don't stop the bleeding."

"Shit, you're right, you're right," James said and moved his long, slender fingers away from his lover's face, pressing them next to Alina's. His hands were still shaking, she could feel his fingers trembling against hers, in fact, his whole body was shaking. The first cry that left his mouth made it sound like he was choking on his grief. Sobs wracked his thin frame, shaking his body with the power of his own anguish. When the tears finally came, they slid down his high cheekbones and dripped from his chin, splattering onto Kieran's chest.

"We have no way to get him out of here," James finally managed to croak. "He's done, it's over."

"Not until he stops breathing. Maybe we could-"

Alina stopped speaking at once when the horrible sounds started coming from Kieran's body. It was a low, gurgling growl, wet and thick. James came alive with movement beside her. Tipping Kieran's body towards them, to the side.

"He's-he's drowning!" He stuttered out. "The bloods choking him." He reached out with a shaking hand and grabbed Kieran's chin, forcing his mouth open. Blood mixed with saliva dribbled down his chin, enough of it for Alina to know they were in trouble, but then Kieran's eyes shot open, revealing the startling blue irises beneath.

His movements were slow and sloppily as he raised his hand from the ground. He reached for his other hand, missed, and reached again, this time he pulled the Ring of Croí free of his middle finger. It was slick with blood. He pressed it against James's chest and spoke one gargled word.

"You."

"Lover, no, you're not thinking straight. I'm no leader and you're not going anywhere. You can't. You can't leave me, lover, because I don't know how to-" James had to stop, the tears were choking him up too much to speak.

Kieran laid his hand flat over James's chest, thumb stroking briefly over his collar bone. He tried to clear his throat, coughed up more phlegm and blood and tried to speak.

"I only trust you," he fought to get the words out of his throat, each one was costing him more effort then anything else he had tried to do in his life. "M'sorry, darlin' I would never choose to leave you, but I don't have a choice. You," he turned his head to the side, spitting thick, clotted wads of blood, "you are the most important person in my life. I think the others could see that. I think, I think they'll follow you."

James hadn't stopped shaking his head, his shoulders hunched up by his ears and shaking. "But I don't think I can do this without you!" He shouted hoarsely.

"You can, one day after...after the next," Kieran pushed out, but he was fading fast. His skin was waxy and so white it almost looked blue. "Live a long life, be happy, and I'll see you in the fields."

"I can't, I can't. I can't!" James screamed, but this time there was no answer. Kieran's body had gone still and cold beneath their fingertips.

"James," Alina tried gently. "James, honey, he's gone." It broke her heart to say the words, it broke her more to admit to herself that it was her fault. *The other half a soul will darken forever*, the words echoed through her mind, *they were never about Darius, they were about Kieran. He never would have been outside this early if I hadn't made him, he would have been safe in the cottage.*

"No, no, no, no," James was muttering, rocking his body back and forth. "I can't-Lina, I can't-"

"I know," she said simply and guided his body to lay across her legs. *Would he even let me be this close once he realized?*

James held Kieran's hand as he cried relentlessly into her denim clad thighs, the fabric growing wet under his face. "I know exactly what you mean," she continued, because she did know what it was like to love someone so much, you honestly didn't know how to live your life without them in it and now because of her, James had lost his.

When James finally pushed himself away from her and sat up on his own, he gently laid Kieran's hand back across his still body. A solemn crowd had gathered around the body. Brigid was back, her face was streaked in blood, not all of it Kieran's. She cleared her throat.

"He didn't pass on the ring, you know the law, that means a vote," she said in a voice that was almost strong.

"He did pass on the ring," Alina blurted.

"Don't tell me he gave it to you, an outsider among us," she spat.

"No, he didn't give it to me," she said quietly.

"Then who..." Brigid began but trailed off as James extended his hand, rotated it until his palm faced the sky, and unfurled his fingers. The Ring of Croí shone like an emerald beacon from his palm and for once it seemed like Brigid didn't have anything to say. Then finally, she nodded her head once.

"The new king," she stated and the few of the Fae that remained echoed her words quietly.

***

James was staring solemnly at his hands and the ring that Brigid had unceremoniously shoved onto his middle finger after they had been scrubbed of blood. He hadn't said a word since it happened. He hadn't wanted to move either, and when Brigid grabbed him to drag him into the cottage, he had screamed, raw and terrible until no more sound had left his throat but a weak gasp for air.

Alina had followed after them, not quite knowing what to do or how to help. She would never forget the sight that met her when she glanced over her shoulder on the way inside. Bodies were being dragged out of tents by the few still living and able-bodied enough to perform such strenuous tasks, and on the road, the black SUV's had rolled into the ditch, they were still running. *I guess Brigid hit her marks after all.*

Alina had watched Brigid scrub James's hands clean of blood and slide the ring almost tenderly on his middle finger. It fit him just as snugly as it did Kieran. The silence that surrounded the three of them was ominous in its stillness, as if they were all waiting for something to happen.

Now, they were still waiting. This time for James to tell them what he wanted to do. The bodies needed burnt, the SUV's needed rid of, the survivors needed seeing to by real medical professionals, but he was still silent despite Brigid's increasingly fervent prodding.

"This can't wait anymore," Brigid said abruptly, rising to her feet, "there's too much that needs doing for the three of us to be sat here like we're made of stone."

"He just saw Kieran *murdered* in front of him!" Alina hissed.

"We all saw it!" Brigid shouted, "we all saw it, but not all of us can afford to mope around like a giant baby about it."

Alina felt her body rearing back as if physically struck by the venom in the other woman's words. "How could you say that?" She asked her quietly, "when you knew what he meant to him."

"He meant a lot to all of us," she said.

"What will you tell them then? He still hasn't

said anything," Alina tried to reason.

"I'm going to lie and give the people the king's orders," she answered.

"And what exactly are the king's orders?" Alina asked, one hand slowly running up and down the length of James's spine.

"To clean up this bloody mess," she said and looked down at her with the most disgust Alina had seen since she first arrived at camp, "is the princess going to leave the tower and help?"

"If you mean me, then the answers no," Alina said flatly, "I don't want to leave him alone right now."

Brigid stormed out in a flurry of flaming hair and swishing skirts and underneath her strong façade, Alina felt their relationship degrading and the loss hurt her deeply. She kept her hands steady and slow up and down his back, tethering James to reality, or at least she hoped so. He still hadn't moved or said a single word.

Hours trickled away slowly, sluggishly, if only she could reach out and catch it in her hands. There was a steady bustle of activity outside the bubble of the cottage, whoever was uninjured was building funeral pyres. The unyielding need to be helpful warred with her guilt, with her refusal to leave James alone, neither of them moved, and so they sat together like statues of grief and guilt as timed passed them by.

An oppressive fog rolled down from the hills and settled low in the valley as the sun began its descent. It was thick and carried a sickly yellow tint in the sun's dying light. She watched from the window as it swallowed the fairy camp and last of Kieran's people whole. Once it had settled, she couldn't even see Brigid and her fiery, loose hair. She couldn't see anything. She may have well have been looking down out of an airplane window over the clouds.

When the sun finally set and blanketed the valley with darkness, the fog seemed to glow ominously white against the black backdrop of the horizon. She almost startled when a red blaze suddenly sparked to life under the cover of the fog. They must be lighting the funeral pyres, the thought struck her suddenly as more of the strange fairy lights began to glow under the cover of fog.

James rose to his feet abruptly and before she could even do as much as call his name, he was rushing purposely down the stairs. Alina followed him at once, sure he was going to do something crazy, half-mad in his grief, *oh god, what if tries to pull Kieran's body off the pyre?*

"James!" She called as he threw open the green painted door and jogged down the steps to the yard. He stormed across the grass and she nearly lost him in the fog when his long legs sent him even farther ahead, but luckily she could see he was heading straight for the largest funeral pyre.

"Oh Kieran," she whispered as she approached the pyre they had built for their king. His body was wrapped in sheets and tied at the ankles, waist, and neck. Sprigs of lavender and thyme were sprinkled generously over the bundle of sheets and surrounding kindling to mask the smell of burning flesh, but they must have only just lighted the pyre, because the flames had yet to reach the body.

The acrid taste of smoke filled her mouth, her lungs, mixing unpleasantly with the damp, thick indescribable taste of fog. Brigid was standing on the opposite side of them, her eyes focused intently on the pyre in front of them. *She must still be angry...* Alina peeked to the side where James was standing incredibly still, watching as the flames crawled closer and closer towards his lover.

"James," she started softly, "are you all right?" She knew it was a stupid question, but she couldn't help but ask it anyway.

"I can't feel a thing," came his monotonous answer and the silence wrapped around them again, broken only by the crackle of the fire as it devoured the pyre of kindling.

She couldn't stand to look at the sight in front of her, so she tried her best to gaze through the cloud of fog and count how many were still among the living.

Four.

Four besides James, Brigid, and herself.

That can't be right... There's no way all the rest all dead.

She spun in a circle, counting the red, hazy glow

of the funeral pyres.

Thirteen.

Thirteen funeral pyres burning in the gloom.

This is really it then, there's seven of us still alive.

Titan's attack had been brutally effective and if the Fae hadn't been on the edge of extinction already, they certainly were now. Even with the families that had abandoned camp before the attack, their numbers were thin.

The other four shadowy figures were moving through the fog towards them and when the fair-haired, ethereal beings emerged from the gloom, Alina could tell from one look of their faces what they were going to say.

They're leaving...

"We're leaving," the tallest on said, Evan, if she remembered correctly.

"Then go," James said coldly.

"Cowards," Brigid muttered darkly under her breath.

Their eyes flicked down to the ring sitting on James's finger and then away. They vanished, the fog swallowing them like they had never been there at all. Near the road, she heard a car start, headlights piercing the cloud of fog, an engine humming loudly, then growing distant as they drove away.

That was it then. They were well and truly on their own.

"I'm not waiting for some bullshit holiday," James said suddenly, with enough passion in his voice to startle her by the sudden change. "I'm going after Titan this weekend. You two can come or not, won't make a difference to me."

His fingers were furled into fists, he shoved them into the pockets of his coat and walked away from the warm blaze back towards the cottage. She watched the stiff set of his spine as he too was devoured by the fog.

CHAPTER 4

The fog had blown over by the time all the pyres had burnt themselves to the ground. Not one of them had gotten any sleep for the rest of the night. They had sat silent and sullen around the dining room table as the pyres burned red through the fog. Alina was contemplating what James had said to them outside and she supposed that Brigid was doing the same.

If he meant what he said, and there was a good chance he did, despite her hopes that it was something that was just said in the grip of grief and fury, then that meant he was going to throw away Kieran's plan in favor of immediate retaliation. Would she help him? Kieran's plan was good, it was smart, but waiting had been a risk, one he ended up paying for with his own life and the lives of so many of his followers.

But if she went with James, there was a good chance they would die. Titan flexed a little, only showed them a portion of their power, and they were wholly unprepared. If they tried to sneak into the headquarters, it would be like sneaking into the lions den. But if she didn't go, she would probably lose the chance forever. There was no way she could do it on her and no way James could make it on his own either, if he went alone he would die.

There wasn't much of a choice at all.

"I'll go," she said softly, breaking the heavy silence that had fallen over them.

"So will I," Brigid said, "I think what you're doing is moronic, even for you, but I follow the king, which I guess is you now."

James nodded his head slowly, "it'll be better with three. Less chance of getting caught without all those other arseholes stomping around."

"How the hell are we going to pull this off?" Brigid asked, "it was bad enough when we had a real king and more people, but what the hell are the three of us supposed to do against a monster like that?"

"We've been going about this all wrong," Alina said, "we've been thinking in terms of using brute force as well as stealth. All we need to do is expose them. Do you think the world's going to react kindly to child experimentation? What about human trafficking? They moved those kids from Ireland to Norway without the parent's consent. All we need is to get in and copy the evidence. Records, paper trails, executive orders, security footage… We make copies of those and we can ruin them."

"That's smart," Brigid agreed begrudgingly, "but that's still going to be risky."

"That doesn't matter!" James snapped, "don't you see that? No matter what we do there's going to be risk. If we go, we might be caught and who the fuck knows what they'd do to us then, but if we stay here and keep hiding in this fucking house they're just going to send more men with more guns and they're going to finish the job. Don't you get it? We're fucked either way so we might as well try. So yes, it's a risk, but we might pull it off. We go in, copy as much shifty shite as we can and get the fuck out."

"What about Darius?"

"What about the children?"

She had Brigid had asked over each other.

"Doesn't matter, once the media gets a hold of all that shite their up to, they'll be strong armed into turning them out," he said.

"You're a selfish bastard, James, I see loss has done nothing to change that," Brigid accused, "I won't leave those kids in there."

"Would you have left Kieran?" Alina asked softly.

"Don't," he warned, his hands folded atop of the table were shaking hard enough to rattle its surface. "Don't you say his name, don't you dare. Not when he'd still be with me if it weren't for you."

So he finally realized...

"How could I have known?" She begged.

"I don't know! But maybe you shouldn't have trusted the word of some creepy dream witch who's been trying to get you away from your friends since this started. Maybe start there, love," he sneered. His eyes drifted towards her shoulder and his mouth was set in a hard frown. "What happened to you?"

"Huh?" She glanced instinctively at her shoulder and saw the frayed edges of the torn fabric stained brown by old blood. "Oh, yeah, I guess I got shot."

"You guess you got shot?" James repeated incredulously. "Jesus Christ, woman, it's been hours and you haven't got that looked at?"

"I didn't really think about it honestly, it doesn't hurt, it's just a little sore," she said.

"Bullshit," Brigid spat and before Alina could defend herself, the other woman was behind her. Brigid took two handfuls of her shirt and pulled. 'Rip'. Alina didn't know whether she was more embarrassed to be half-naked in front of these two or disappointed that her shirt was so flimsy.

"Hey!" She protested and curled an arm around her breasts to preserve some sense of modesty.

"Oh please, spare us the false dignity," Brigid rolled her eyes, "no one in this rooms gives a shite about your tits."

"Ow! Could you at least be gentle?" She asked as the other woman began prodding her wound with her fingers. Alina could see the uncertainty etched into Brigid's face and it made a sudden surge of nervousness take hold of her, speeding up her heart, and raising goosebumps along her arms.

"What? What is it? If it's something really bad

just tell me now," she demanded.

"It's nothing bad, at least I don't think so. The bullet wound looks cauterized, both on the entry and exit wounds. Did you do this yourself?" She asked.

"I don't think so, I don't remember, that was around the same time that-well, things happened really fast after that," she tried to explain, avoiding looking anywhere near James.

"So now you can self-cauterize? Why the hell didn't you try something like that on him?" James demanded.

"How could I when I didn't even know I could do it?" She snapped.

"He was too far gone, and you know it, so just leave her be," Brigid said with finality and the subject was officially dropped.

"So how the hell are we going to get to Oslo? We don't have the connections we used to," Brigid asked while Alina tried to cover herself back up with the tattered remains of her shirt.

"I know someone," James said, "he should be near Galway. If I can get a hold of him, he should be able to be here by tomorrow morning."

"Who is he?" Alina asked.

"My brother, Oliver, he runs one of those Cliff's of Moher cruises for the tourists. We can use his boat," James said.

"Won't he ask questions?" Brigid asked, "we really don't need to drag an outsider into this mess."

"He owes me," James said and looked towards the stairs. She didn't miss the haunted look that he sent them and remembered how Kieran had carried him down just yesterday. It seemed like a lifetime ago.

James dragged himself up from the table and she saw the faint trembling in his hands, "we should try and get a couple hours of sleep." But he didn't go up the stairs, instead, he threw himself onto the couch, folding his arms across his chest. And wasn't that familiar? How long had it taken her to go back to sleeping in the bed she had shared with Darius?

"I'm going to stay in the cottage tonight," Brigid said, breaking the thick silence that had fallen between them. "I don't want to go back out there."

"Yeah, of course, I mean, it's not like it's my house or anything. You can do what you want," Alina stuttered, unsure how to speak to her after the tension that had risen between them before Kieran's funeral.

"No, it isn't," Brigid agreed, "it's his now," she said with a jerk of the head towards James.

"Right," she replied awkwardly, "well, I'm just going to bed now." Alina fled upstairs, holding the scraps of her shirt against her chest.

The first thing she did was lock herself in the bathroom and examine her shoulder with her own two eyes. The skin was mottled and darkened by an intense heat source, that much she could see for herself. Brigid and James had described it as being cauterized but it looked different than she expected, maybe because the heat source came from within her instead of externally. Her fingers brushed over the rough, scaly patch of skin and winced. That was going to be an ugly scar, but it was better than ending up on one of those pyres.

She found a bottle of rubbing alcohol in the wooden cabinet above the sink and cleaned carefully around the exit and entry wounds. She probably didn't have to, the heat most likely killed any bacteria that had been close to the wound, but she needed something to do with her hands while her mind was still racing. She wasn't ready to go to sleep, going to sleep meant that everything that had happened had been real, going to sleep meant that she wasn't going to wake up from this nightmare.

When she crawled into her bed and drew the covers over her head, she was inexplicably reminded of the first night she spent without Darius. But unlike tonight, she hadn't been alone then, she had been sandwiched between Kieran and James on a bed that was much too small for three grown adults. The tears that spilled wet and hot down her cheeks were a surprise, so were the sobs that escaped her gasping mouth. The grief hit her hard and shocked her by its sudden appearance and strength. She spent so long trying to keep James together that she forgot to give herself time to mourn.

The sound of her cries echoed loudly in the

sleeping cottage, so she covered her mouth to stifle the noise, but she could still hear it. The sound of someone crying, alone in a dark house. She listened carefully and could still hear it, it sounded like it was coming from downstairs. *Oh James...* She debated for a few seconds if he'd even welcome her presence downstairs, but knew from experience that sometimes it was best if the people you cared about didn't let you be alone even if you yourself think that's what you needed.

She shoved the covers off her and padded quietly downstairs and into the living room. James had turned on his side, facing the back of the couch, his whole body was shaking. She made her way carefully to him and nudged the small of his back.

"Budge up," she whispered and for a few long seconds he didn't answer her, but then he scooted closer towards the back of the sofa and she squeezed in beside him, wrapping her arms around his waist to anchor herself from sliding off the cushions.

He still wept, for a long while he wept and shook and made pathetic noises, but she held him all the while, crying her own salty tears into the space between his shoulder blades. At some point the cries tapered off and he fell into a restless sleep, protected and cradled in her arms. She nuzzled her face into his strong back and let sleep swallow her away.

CHAPTER 5

His blaring presence was almost suffocating in the little cottage kitchen. It wasn't that he was loud or obnoxious like James, no, he hadn't said a single word since he walked in. But he walked with confidence and a lazy elegance, like he couldn't be bothered to be weighed down by the atmosphere or the company he kept. When he walked past her to their rickety table, it was as if the shadows parted for him, a halo of sunlight accentuating his overly bright smile and warm, tan skin.

He was about as tall as James, maybe a hair taller, and although they both possessed the same lean, long limbs, it seemed like Oliver kept a little more toned. His hair was artfully tousled, each brown curl carefully sculpted around his angular face. He pulled a chair out for himself and loosened the knot of his tie, winking when he caught Alina's eyes on him.

"I know I'm probably overdressed, but I came straight from a work meeting," he explained smoothly in an accent that was thicker than James's, and more familiar, *Yorkshire* her brain supplied. He shook a cigarette out from a pack he slid seamlessly out of his trouser pocket and popped the end between his lips, he lit it with practiced ease, and inhaled, sighing the smoke out of his nose.

"Cut the shite, *Oli,*" James said, stressing the overfamiliar nickname. It wasn't hard to believe the two brothers didn't get along. "You overcharge tourists to take them to the Cliff's of Moher on your yacht. That's not exactly what I would call a business meeting, would you?"

"Careful, Jimmy-boy, did you drag me all the way out here to insult me? Because by the looks of the carnage outside, you need my help with something," he said, lazy curls of smoke caressing his jawline and perfuming that perfect hair with heavy scent of tobacco.

Brigid leaned against the counter, pretty, petite nose wrinkled, lips slightly pursed in distaste, "yeah, I don't really fancy working with this prick. He's even worse than you," she said to James.

"Aw, darlin', you're breaking my heart. Pretty bird like you, it'd be a shame if we got off on the wrong foot," Oliver crooned and stamped his cigarette out on the dining room table. "Now, why did you bring me out here, baby brother? And why does it look like a deranged circus clown murdered an entire village outside?"

"Because someone murdered a village outside," James snapped, and his brother shrugged.

"Sounds like a problem for the garda then, why

call me?" He asked then suddenly jabbed a finger in his direction, "unless you were the one that did it."

"I didn't fucking do it! I would never-" he stopped, voice too thick with emotion.

Oliver's eyes flicked from side to side, taking in the room, "why isn't Kieran here breathing down your neck like usual?"

James stood abruptly and left the room. His feet thundered up the stairs and a door slamming shut echoed in the dining room. Oliver shrugged, lighting a second cigarette.

"Did he finally leave him then? I always knew he would, my brother's an acquired taste," he said.

"Kieran's dead," Brigid said coldly, and Alina couldn't hide her shock when Oliver burst out laughing then coughing as he inhaled abruptly on his cigarette.

"So, the little fag finally got what he deserved, huh?" He asked. "Shame I wasn't here to see it."

'Thud'. The hilt of one of Brigid's throwing knives embedded into the edge of the wooden table, a little farther over and it would have missed the edge of the table entirely and hit his crotch.

"Jesus Christ, woman!" His chair scraped back along the floor as he skittered back. "Are you mad? You could have taken my cock off with that!"

Brigid leaned towards him, palms planted on the tabletop, the smile of her face was feral, "if you ever say that word in my presence or insult the-

Kieran again, I *will* take your cock off. But I'll do it slowly, and, when I'm done, I'll make you fucking eat it," she promised. She stared him down for several long seconds before she too was storming away, fiery hair swishing angrily down her shoulders and back as she took the stairs two at a time.

"Jesus, it usually takes me at least two whiskeys before I can clear a room like that," he said too brightly for a man who'd just been threatened with dismemberment.

"What you said was completely uncalled for," Alina scolded, "a man died here last night, the love of your brother's life. Even if you have a problem with his lifestyle, the least you could do is show some respect, for your brother's sake."

"I don't need a lecture in manners from a mouthy little bird," he said.

"Well, you need one from someone," she said and rose to leave, but his hand shot out, grabbing her by the arm.

"If you leave me here all by my lonesome, I'm just going to turn tail and leave," he warned her, "and I still reckon you need me."

She lowered herself back down to her seat and plucked his cigarette out of his hand, she brought it to her lips and inhaled deeply, feeling the burn race down her throat and flood her lungs. She had to clamp down on the urge to immediately start coughing. *Jesus, has it really been that long since I quit smoking?* She released the smoke from her mouth in a long, careful sigh and peered through the ribboning gray wall of smoke at the man sitting across from her. He really was handsome; it was a shame that he was such an asshole.

"James is my best friend," she admitted. "He thought you could help us, and we could really use it, but I'm not going to be around anyone that talks about the people he loves like that."

"Shame, love, because I enjoy surrounding myself with beautiful birds," Oliver said, winking as he took his cigarette back, his fingers caressing her knuckles as he pulled his hand away.

She snatched her hand away, "I'm taken."

"I hate that word," he told her with a wolfish smile, "I prefer my women to feel free. Free with their bodies, free with their affections…"

"I'm committed, not enslaved," she corrected.

"If you say so, now how about you tell me why I'm here and I promise I won't disparage my baby brother's 'lifestyle'" he said, fingers making air quotes around the word lifestyle.

"We need to get to Oslo, as under the radar as possible, and if you have a boat-"

"A yacht," he corrected.

"A yacht, fine, if you have a yacht then I'm fairly certain he wants you to get us there," she finished.

"To Oslo?" He questioned.

"To Oslo," she confirmed.

"From Galway? On a yacht? Are you all fucking mad?" He asked, stamping his cigarette out on the table, and flicking the butt away with his thumb and index finger.

She couldn't help the wry grin that stole over her face, "you should have seen what we got here on."

"So, you're serious then. This really isn't some stupid prank? Because sometimes James can be a little prick," he said.

"We're serious and we'll pay you everything we can," she said.

He leaned over the table, one eyebrow cocked, interest piqued, "and how much exactly is everything?"

She thought about the money she glimpsed in the floor safe when Kieran had opened it one day after their training and the stacks of notes she saw in there. She wasn't James and she wasn't Brigid, so she probably didn't have the authority to offer him anything, but James wanted revenge and she wanted Darius, and the Fae were broken, the survivors scattered, what would they need it for?

"What would you say to 20,000?" She asked. She only got a quick glimpse, but if there was anything she knew, it was money.

"I'd say you have a deal, darlin', I'll get you to Oslo, bloody hell, I'd get you into Russia for that," he said.

"We're leaving immediately, so don't get too comfortable," she warned him.

"Comfortable? In this shithole? I wouldn't dream of it, love," he said.

She took the stairs two at a time, it was a testament to Kieran's training that she didn't even feel the slightest bit winded, but before she could knock on James and Kieran's bedroom door, she noticed that the door to her own room was cracked open. One peek inside confirmed that James was pacing restlessly beside the end of her bed, looking more like an agitated leopard in a cage.

"James?" She called hesitantly, "I talked to your brother-"

"Don't call him that," he spat, "that man's no brother of mine."

"Fine, Oliver then, I talked to Oliver and he'll get us to Oslo," she told him.

"What did you offer him? Because I can guarantee that he won't do it for nothing," he said.

"I offered him twenty grand," she said honestly and watched his expression slacken with shock.

"And where in the hell do you expect to get that kind of money when you've been locked out of your accounts?" He asked incredulously.

"The floor safe, the one in Kieran's old office. I saw him open it once, so I have a pretty good idea what's in there," she said.

"You promised him Kieran's money?"

"Well, it's yours now, isn't it?" She asked bluntly, "besides, it's our only way to get to Oslo under Titan's nose, unless you have another brilliant idea?"

"Don't tell Brigid," he begged instead, and she agreed.

***

CHAOS AND FLAMES

The yacht was like any Alina had the privilege to be on in her old life. Those parties with the music, pulsing lights, flutes of champagne, it was worlds away from the place she thought of as home now. The sleepy white cottage nestled snugly against the rolling emerald hills and rocky crags that dominated the wild Irish landscape with its rickety dining room table and dreadful checkered curtains, that was where her heart ached to return to. But it wasn't the cottage itself she yearned to return to, it was the memories that place guarded, the feelings she harbored there.

Somewhere along this journey she had changed, the wealth and finery she had always thought were the key to her happiness had been replaced by a ragtag group of people. They had become her home and they were what her heart ached to return to. Darius, his strength, his unwavering love, even his oddly endearing way of speaking, though it dated him immediately; Brigid, her love burned the hottest, quick to anger, but even quicker to bleed for the few she called family; James, who loved the hardest and was quick to hurt, who threw up walls built with dry humor and sass, who pretended to care about nothing and no one, but was probably the one who cared the most; and Kieran, who she would never see again while she was on this earth, who's death would haunt her nightmares until her last great sleep.

These people were her family, her home, and it was likely that when this was all said and done that at least half those people wouldn't be on speaking terms with her. What was worse than to steal the collective fortune of an entire group of people and give it to a bigoted asshole? Probably not much, but at least she and James were on the same page when it came to taking the money. Sometimes you had to do bad in order to do good, but she knew as soon as she started thinking like that and making excuses for herself, it usually meant that whatever she had done was wrong.

James had sequestered himself in the bedroom and hadn't said a word to his brother since he welcomed them on board. Brigid was similarly brooding in a corner by herself, meaning Alina was the only one left to keep the peace with Oliver and make sure the arrogant captain kept them on course. She could put up with his flirting a little better, maybe even welcome it as a distraction, if he weren't just a generally terrible person. A beautiful exterior, but rotten inside, and whenever he opened his mouth, that rot bled through.

She was currently perched on the edge of the captain's bed where James had seemed to take up permanent residence for their last journey together. Her hand rested on the base of his spine, a warm, comforting presence. He hadn't slept a whole night through since Kieran was murdered and it was beginning to show in the hollow, exhausted way he held himself when he was awake. He wasn't eating properly either and for someone who didn't have a lot of weight to lose, the fat he was shedding was starting to give him a haunting, skeletal appearance.

"You should try to eat something," she said.

"If I do, you get to scrub the vomit out of the sheets," he replied sullenly.

"James, I can't imagine what you're going through, but you have to start trying to live. You're letting yourself waste away."

"How can I?" He asked her seriously, "how can I when he's not here with me?"

"You have to find the strength to keep going," she begged. "One day at a time, one hour at a time, one second even, but you have to find that in yourself, I can't do it for you."

"Maybe I don't want to find it," he muttered.

"He would be devastated if he could see you like this," she said.

"He would pitch a fit for sure," James agreed easily, "but he's not here."

"No," she said, "no, he's not."

She got unsteadily to her feet, still unused to the roll and sway of the boat over the water. She leaned over the mattress and pressed her lips to his limp, bottle-blond head.

"Try to sleep," she murmured and let herself out of the bedroom and onto the deck. She folded her arms around herself, skin tightening as the first brisk wave of wind misted her with the Atlantic. The sun was setting on the horizon, casting twin sunsets against the sky and the shimmering water.

Smoke swirled in a lazy circle from her left and she wasn't surprised she didn't hear him approach her over the roar of the ocean and the hum of the yacht's engine. The soft yellow and orange lighting and dark wood of the yacht's deck would have made for a romantic setting if it had been with anyone other than the person she was standing next to.

His overly cheerful voice interrupted the calm atmosphere, "so, are you ready to explain to me why my baby brother is wearing the ring that belongs to the king of the Fae?"

The shock that swept over her was akin to being hit with a bucket of ice water. She could hear her heartbeat thumping in her ears, her fingers felt like immoveable blocks of ice. Her voice sounded too high when she finally answered him.

"How do you know?"

"You really think I didn't recognize that cottage? That property's only been the seat of the king since the Roman's thought the sun would never set on their empire," he said.

"But how do you know about any of that?" She asked urgently, "Kieran said the humans don't know about them, so how could you know any of that?"

She stilled in amazement as a little sphere of water rose from over the side of the railing and transformed into a butterfly shape that unfurled its wings and floated towards her. She shrieked when it suddenly burst near her face, drenching the front of her shirt with water.

Oliver was nearly bent double by the great guffaws of laughter that consumed him, he wiped tears from the corners of his warm, brown eyes, "oh love, you've got to smile more often, it's a great look on you."

And when she raised her fingers to her face, she found was smiling, for the first time since Kieran's death, she was smiling. She tried to ring out the front of her shirt over the railing, casting a glance down to see his handsome visage reflected in the water next to her. His reflection wiggled his fingers at her in the water.

"Mum had an affair with a water nymph," was all he said in explanation.

"I guess Kieran's uncle was right about James after all, he isn't fully human," she said and turned back around to face him fully. "Why doesn't James know what he is?"

"Because Mum was a whore," he said simply, shrugging one shoulder, "we weren't sure if he actually was from the same bloke or not."

He stamped his dwindling cigarette out on the railing, "figures, not only did he have to be a fag but now he's the king of the enemy."

Her hand shot out and shoved the center of his chest, using the strength that now came easily to her. His arms pinwheeled as he lurched several steps back, he leveled a glare at her as soon as he regained his balance.

"Jesus woman, what the hell was that for?" He

asked.

"Brigid already told you not to call him that, don't make her tell you again," she warned.

"To bad he'll never have the balls to go for you," he lamented, "you're a little firecracker, eh?"

"You have no idea," she told him and folded her arms over her chest. "Don't you care about him at all?"

"He's my blood, for whatever that's worth," he offered.

"Apparently that's not worth much to you," she said and tried to brush past him back into the captain's quarters, but he caught her by the elbow.

"And why are you working yourself up about it? Hm?" He asked, his grip firm but not painful.

"He's my best friend, my family," she told him and shook his hand off her body.

"Then my little brother must be the luckiest fella there is," he said.

"And whys that?"

"To have a pretty thing like you get so worked up on his behalf," he said and for the first time that evening she noticed how closely he was speaking to her. His body was angled towards her, his head tipped down, his warm lips brushing the shell of her ear. Today he was wearing black pleated pants that screamed expensive and a long-sleeved white button down with the top few buttons undone.

She almost rolled her eyes despite herself, trust Oliver to dress up when the rest of them had been wearing the same change of clothes for the last two nights. He hadn't said anything else to her, but he hadn't moved away either, just watched her without a blink; his smirk carved into his face. She levelled her gaze at him and tried to take a step back, away from his body and the heat it radiated.

"I'm taken, and even if I weren't, I wouldn't ever go for a gaudy asshole like you," she said hotly.

"Oh?" He purred, the words dripping from his mouth, "because I notice you watching me quite a lot."

"Watching someone and noticing someone are two very different things," she said, but to her horror her body was responding to his. She could feel a fire burning in her blood when he leaned closer and her heart was beating a little faster than she would have liked.

His lips brushed mockingly against the shell of her ear and when he spoke again, his voice was low and taunting, "is it?"

Before she could say anything, he tipped his head just so and forced their lips together. Her heart felt like it was in her throat and when her mouth parted in surprise, Oliver slipped his tongue between her lips and then they were kissing properly. Their tongues slid together sinuously, and she felt a familiar fire light in her belly as they kissed and kissed and kissed. Unthinkingly, she slid her hand into his hair and felt the smooth brown locks slipping between her fingers.

They parted for a brief second as they both tried to catch their breath but then he was all over her again. Hands squeezing the outsides of her thighs, tongue in mouth, teeth nipping her lips. Her own hands were everywhere, clutching his broad shoulders, running down his chest, fingers skimming the ridges of his abs through his white button down. His fingers dug into her hips, dragging her impossibly closer until they were pressed flush together. She could feel her own moans vibrating in between their sealed lips and oddly enough, that was what woke her from this arousal fueled escapade.

She got her hands between their bodies and pushed him firmly away, crossing her arms over her chest to put a physical barrier between them.

"What is it? What's wrong, love?" He asked and just like she predicted, tried to pull her back in.

She held her hand out, pressing firmly on his chest, "I told you already that I have someone. So, this," she gestured between their bodies, "isn't going to happen."

"You weren't saying that a minute ago," he said, his smirk set on his lips.

"No, but I'm saying it now and that's all that matters," she told him firmly.

"Love, come on, you don't mean that. Now why don't you c'mere," he said and reached for her one more time. Her heart was pounding in her chest, all she could do was relive what happened the last time she was alone on a ship with a man who wouldn't take no for an answer. It hadn't really been that long at all since Vane had tried to force himself on her and now it looked like it was going to happen again. She could the liquid fire igniting under her skin, gathering in her palms and in the soles of her feet, ready to run or to defend herself.

"Oi!"

The shout scared both of them, startling them further apart.

For the first time since they boarded, James was outside the cabin. He was in the rumpled clothes that he walked on board in and his slight body looked like it would topple with the first strong gust of wind, but there was still a strength in him that made his tall figure appear imposing.

"What the hell, man?" He asked Oliver, "you're so desperate for it you have to try and force yourself on a poor bird?"

Oliver scoffed, "poor bird? You should have seen her a few minutes ago, she was all over me."

"Well, she's not now," he said and walked towards them, slinging an arm over Alina's shoulders. She heard him hiss under his breath when their skin made contact and started taking deeper breaths to get herself back under control. Despite the heat rising from her body, he never let her go, just guided her around towards the cabin. He tipped his head back, addressing his brother.

"After all this time, I thought you'd be better at fucking off when you're not wanted," he tossed back over his shoulder and shut the door, cutting off Oliver's reply. He dropped his arm from her shoulder, brow furrowed as he studied the skin.

"Ow, fuck, I think you burnt me," he mumbled but before she apologized, he flopped back onto the bed, lifting one of his arms out. "You coming or what?" He asked and she crawled onto the bed, slipping gratefully beneath his arm.

She listened to his breathing even out, his strong, steady heart gradually lulling her to sleep. She had forgotten for a moment, even with Vane, she hadn't been alone then either.

CHAPTER 6

Oliver docked in the middle of the night, and Brigid rented them an unassuming little car as soon as they got ashore. All in all, it took a lot less time then Alina thought and before she knew it, she was staring at the sleek, modern lines of the Titan headquarters as it cut through the rich city skyline. Sunday night, after dark, it wasn't as deserted as a bank holiday like Kieran had originally wanted, but the lights in most of the offices were out and the parking garage was virtually empty.

Brigid was standing back at the trunk, strapping knives in easy to conceal places along her body. She was dressed like the night in dark blues and blacks, her red hair braided carefully away from her face. She leveled them with a single, determined stare.

"The two of you don't know a thing about computers, do you?" She asked suddenly.

"Never had enough money to own one, babe."

"I had an i.t. department on call," Alina admitted.

"Yeah, that's what I thought," she said and

sighed heavily. "You two will have to go down to the lab by yourselves, find the kids, find Darius, and get the hell out."

"Wait, wait, wait," James said, "and what will you be doing while we're doing the heavy lifting? Taking a nap?"

"I'm going up," she pointed with her index finger, "the bigger the office, the more incriminating evidence will be on the computer. Someone has to approve all this shit," she reasoned, and Alina found herself nodding.

"She's right, the managers will have all the documentation we need to shut Titan down for good," she admitted, "but do you know how to copy the files onto a USB?"

"How simple do you think I am?" Brigid retorted, "everyone knows how to do that."

Alina didn't give her the satisfaction of admitting that she was exception to the rule. Brigid shut the trunk of their car and handed each of them the slim handle of a sheathed knife.

"I'll take care of the night guard, but there's nothing I can do about the security cameras. You both understand that means we have to be fast, right? I don't know who monitors those, but once they bring in reinforcements, we're done."

"We know," Alina reassured her, but Brigid was still watching them with a troubled expression.

"Stay safe," she finally said, "and give me a five-minute head start."

"We will," she said, "and Brigid, we'll see you

back out here and we'll have everyone with us, I promise."

Things may have still been strained between them since Kieran's death, but they were still connected. That connection had been frayed and was wrought with tension, but nothing could erase that first laugh they had together or the trauma they shared. As Titan loomed above them like a sleeping giant, all they really had was each other. Brigid nodded her head in acknowledgement and then slipped into the shadows as if she had been born there. Alina reached out blindly and grasped James's hand, clasping it tightly.

"We can do this, can't we?" She asked him softly.

His answering smile was full of false confidence and did nothing to reassure her.

***

The basement of Titan headquarters was a maze of sterile, white hallways and buzzing fluorescent lights. Whether or not they made it to be disorienting, they succeeded. It was just James and Alina, Brigid was still upstairs in the offices, trying to copy as much incriminating information as she could onto a flash drive. If there was a way they could ensure that Titan fell to its knees, it was that. The media would have a field day with the illegal child experimentation alone.

There were doors with glass windows that lined the hallway, but a quick glance inside confirmed they were still in the animal testing zone. The lights were bright, the halls and little rooms deserted, and their footsteps echoed against the clean, white tiles on the floor. Their fingers were still intertwined when they found the first child.

He was as white as the sheets he was tucked under, a few wisps of dark hair framing his cherubic face. He couldn't have been any older than four, though the machines he was hooked up to made him look smaller than he was. James squeezed her hand tightly.

"Oh God, we found them," he whispered and when she looked at him, she found he wasn't looking in the same room as she was, his eyes were glued on the glass door of the room across the hall and when she looked inside, she saw the other three. The twins, and their beautiful, fragile wings folded against their backs, and the other boy, his fine, silver hair as long as he was tall. They were all connected to similar machines and with dawning horror, Alina noticed that they weren't injecting them with anything, they were pulling blood *out*.

"What the hell are you two doing standing there like you've been turned to stone?" Brigid asked, "we have to *hurry*."

James mutely pointed to the room and Brigid's eyes followed, a soft gasp leaving her when her eyes found the kids. "it's really them."

"Did you copy the files already?" Alina asked and Brigid wiggled the USB at her in confirmation.

"Help me get them out, quick," Brigid ordered and they all three split up, gently pulling out IV's and unhooking wires from the unconscious children. The Fae blood burned through the sedative fast when it was no longer being continuously pumped into their bodies, and by the time Brigid was slicing through the ties that kept them chained to their beds, the children were beginning to wake and try to move around.

They seemed to recognize Brigid as one of their own and congregated around her like a squad of ducklings. Brigid counted heads and made sure they had all four, pinching cheeks and chuffing chins as she did.

"Can you all walk?" She asked them and received sleepy nods in return. She glanced at Alina and James; her arms spread protectively around the group of children gathered around her legs. Alina knew what she would say before she said it.

"I'm getting them out of here," she said, "you can come with me or keep looking."

Alina couldn't blame her, the kids were her priority and she respected that, but her priority was with Darius and she couldn't leave until she found him. James gave Brigid a mock salute.

"Get them outta here, Cap'n, we still have some business with Titan, don't we Lins?"

Alina nodded and took his hand, squeezing it gratefully, "we do."

"I'll come back if I can. Don't do anything stupid," she warned them.

Then James was pulling her deeper into the lab, head jerking from side to side as he peered into each little room. She didn't know how long they were searching for, each second felt like it lasted a lifetime, but isn't that always the case when you're fixated on time?

James stopped suddenly, the breath pushed out of him in one sudden exhale, "Jesus Christ, there he is."

Alina threw herself against the glass window, neck craned to the side to get a glimpse of him. He was unconscious and from her angle, it almost looked like he was sleeping peacefully. His auburn hair was unwashed and hung in clumps around his face and spilled out over his pillow. A smattering of stubble painted his cheeks and chin, trailing down his jaw to the thick steel collar they had clamped over his throat. There was a cord of chain wrapped around his waist and another around his legs, both wrists and ankles were shackled to the metal observation table.

James whistled, "well, they didn't want him going anywhere, did they? Pretty stupid on their part though."

"What do you mean?" Alina asked as she tried the door handle and found it unlocked.

"Well you can just melt it right off him, can't you? You know, with your fire thing," he said and wiggled his fingers at her.

They eased through the door and shut it quietly behind them. They came to stand on opposite sides of Darius's bedside and methodically began unhooking him from the medical equipment that loomed over his head. Alina pulled out his IV, it looked like they had him on a stronger sedative then the one the children were on.

"We're all clear on my side," James said and took a step away from the bed. At her questioning look, he explained, "well, if it's anything like those kids then his body is going to burn through that sedative fast and I know the big guy pretty well, he'll be ready to fight until his brain catches up with his muscles."

"Right," she muttered and summoned the familiar heat to her palms. She started at his feet and gradually melted his bindings until the metal binding him was no more than a shiny, hardening sludge pooling on the tile floor. *I guess I should be grateful he can't be burned either, this never would have worked with anyone else*, she mused as she melted the metal collar around his throat.

She had no more than gotten his neck free when he startled and jerked awake. Just as James had predicted, his large, muscular body was almost moving on its own. He rolled off the metal table and instinctually swung his arm out, as if warding off a physical blow. Unlike James, she hadn't been smart enough to get out of the way and her lover's arm connected painfully with her midriff and she was flung from her feet. James used his own body to cushion the spot she would have crashed to against the wall and though she felt the breath leave him at the impact, they both managed to stay on their feet.

"Would you calm down?" James asked wildly,

"or would you like to throw your girlfriend around a bit more?"

His words seemed to break through to Darius who looked like he had been ready to transform right here in this little exam room. He shook his head and then his emerald eyes were focused on hers and the rest of the world melted away.

"My Lina," he muttered gruffly, his voice scratchy with disuse.

She felt James's arms fall away from her as she ran to him. She barreled into him a little harder than she intended, but he still caught her easily, sweeping her off her feet. Their mouths met for the first time in weeks, but it may have well been for the first time for all that it felt like a charge was lit between them. Every nerve ending in her body was set alight, chills tightened the skin on her arms, swept down her spine, and curled her toes inside her boots as he cupped her face in his warm, large hands.

"My Lina," he rumbled after they were forced to part for air, "you should not have come for me, it's far to dangerous in this place."

"There's no world, no universe, or parallel dimension where I could have left you here," she told him and pressed upward to kiss him again. Being held by him was like feeling the rain sliding down your skin after weeks of drought, she couldn't get enough, she needed to be closer.

"Yeah, hate to interrupt, but in case you're forgetting, we're still in the basement of crazy town here and we might really need to, I don't know, get the fuck out," James interjected.

Darius broke their kiss and set her carefully back down on two feet, "James!" He exclaimed exuberantly, "I'm surprised Alina was able to part you from your other half, where is Kieran?"

The color drained from his face until James looked as white as the tiles beneath their shoes. He walked out of the exam room and back into the hall, slamming the door shut behind him. The silence that followed was almost obnoxious.

"He's gone Darius," she finally said when she could see the question in his eyes. "Kieran's dead, Titan...they murdered him and most of the encampment."

"If they dare hurt the people I put under my protection I will pay them back tenfold," he warned but she laid her hand soothingly over his arm.

"Darius, no. It's over. Brigid already has everything we need to bring Titan down, all we need to do now is get out before we get caught," she told him gently and took his hand in hers. "Let's just go and leave this place behind us."

"As you wish, Lina," Darius agreed easily and opened the door for her, but she tugged him along and they left the exam room together. The latch to the door clicked shut behind them when she noticed James standing stiffly in the middle of the wide hallway.

"Nice of you two to join the party," he said sardonically.

"Party?" She asked but he didn't need to answer, because at that same exact moment, both she and Darius saw the gun. It was currently pointed at James who stood a few feet ahead of them, but the shaking hand that held it, jerked it towards Alina, then Darius, then back to James.

"Nobody moves! I mean it, no one moves. Anybody-Anybody moves, and I start shooting!"

CHAPTER 7

Simon Aldridge was a snake possessing a man's body. His eyes shifted side to side, tongue flicking out to nervously coat his lips as he held them at gun point. The arm holding the gun was trembling. He obviously wasn't used to holding all the power in a room. Darius could see it too, Alina could see the subtle shift in his positioning, the cords of muscle stiffening as if he were readying himself to spring.

Simon looked exactly like she remembered him, the same thinning salt and pepper hair, the same leering eyes, the same aura of perpetual nervousness. From her experience dealing with him back in New York, he was the last person she would ever have expected to be holding them at gunpoint. He must have been demoted after she got Darius out of New York, they probably had him watching the security cameras.

She jerked her head to the side, talking quietly and slowly so not to startle Simon's trigger finger. "Darius," she warned. Simon may be inexperienced with a weapon, but one lucky shot would be all it took to end one of their lives.

As soon as she spoke, Simon swiveled, and that gun was pointed directly at her now. "Don't move! Stay right where you are, bitch, I will kill you. I will!"

"This is just embarrassing, mate, the way you're shaking that thing around I think the ceilings in more danger than we are," James said and Simon swiveled again, the barrel was staring down James's chest now.

"I said shut up! All of you just shut up."

"Actually, and I do hate to correct you, I really do, but you didn't actually say anything about keeping quiet, you said not to move and I am not moving," James pointed out.

"Don't mock him, James," Alina begged. There was a way to get out of this, but not if the two idiots she had with her got themselves shot first.

"I'm not mocking him, I'm really not," he skipped a step forward and all four people in the room collectively held their breath, but no shot ever came. Simon's arm was really quivering now, and she could see the barrel of the gun bobbing up and down.

"I just think he's a gutless piece of shite who won't ever pull that trigger," he continued and hopped another step forward.

"I'm warning you!" Simon shouted and the gun bopped and weaved in his quaking grip.

At the same time Darius interjected, "I would be wary, James."

"No, I don't think I will 'be wary,' whatever the

fuck that's supposed to mean," he leapt another foot forward, the grin stretching his face could be described as anything but friendly. It was the grin of a man who was teetering on the edge of sanity.

"What I think is that we have evidence of Titan being creepy and genuinely fucked up, I think Brigid is sending those files to every major news team she can find, and I think I can walk right up to this scrawny little arsehole who sent his goons to kill my-" he paused and then continued softly, "my everything, and take the gun right out of his limp wristed hand. That is what I think, Lina-cakes." He punctuated this with another big step in Simon's direction, this brought him directly in front of the shorter man, so close that the guns barrel was pressed snugly against his chest.

"I-I'm warning you," Simon said uselessly, but even Alina could tell that he was done. He was never going to pull the trigger.

James curled his hand around the top of the gun and began pressing the barrel down and away from his chest. His smile was biting and mocking all at once.

"There, just let go, now doesn't that feel better you useless sack of shite?"

Simon's face twisted unbelievably with sudden rage, he pushed the barrel hard against James's stomach, and pulled the trigger. The shot was deafening as it bounced off the walls of the hall and when the noise faded and all Alina was left with was a ringing in her ears, Darius sprung forward. His hand was outstretched, ready to throw Simon away from James, Alina also moved forward, the need to reach James overwhelming her every pore, but James was the one that surprised her the most. He hadn't moved, he didn't fall, he didn't even scream, instead, his hand shot out and curled viciously around Simon's throat. The Ring of Croí glinted like a sudden emerald wink of light on his ring finger as he curled his hand into a fist and crushed Simon's throat.

James watched Simon's face turn blue and then white before he dropped the body. It was only when Simon hit the tiled floor with a dull 'thud' that he seemed to come aware of his own injuries. One long fingered hand came to clutch at his stomach and the blood that bubbled from the wound, the other hung limply at his side.

"Huh," the sound that left his mouth was halfway between a puzzled sigh and a barked laugh.

Darius and Alina reached him just as he was falling back and for the second time in her life, Alina found herself diving to catch someone she cared about. She didn't make it this time either, but Darius did. He held James in strong, steady arms and lowered him gently to the floor. Alina's hands covered James's own as she applied pressure to the wound. Her heart was pounding in her throat, her fingers became wet and slick with blood. *There's so much blood, this can't happen again, not again.* She couldn't let this happen again.

She pulled her hands back and focused heat into

her right palm. "I'm going to cauterize the wound so the bleeding stops, it should buy us enough time to get you to a hospital," she explained gently. "You have to move your hand, James."

James shook his head weakly, "don't, Lina, it's not what I want." He spoke in a calm, rational voice despite the blood that was pouring out of him and the pain he must be in.

"What the hell are you talking about?" She asked furiously. "We don't have time for a debate! Darius, I need you to restrain him, this will hurt." She paused when her lover made no move to do as she instructed. "Darius!"

"It's not what he wants, Lina, he wants to leave this earth." Darius said.

"No! He doesn't just get to decide that! That's not how this works! He can't just-just give up. You can't leave us, James, that's not what Kieran wanted for you." She finished softly.

James laughed quietly though it seemed to cause him great pain to do so. "I never listened to that short little bastard before, why would I start just because he's gone?" James turned his serious eyes towards her, reaching out and intertwining their blood slick hands. "I couldn't do it without him, Lina, I'm a coward. It's better this way, it's what I want."

"What about me? What about me you jackass!?" She shouted and gripped his hand fiercely tight. A sudden rush of hot tears flooded her eyes. "You think it's going to be easy for me to live without you when-when," she had to stop and swallow down the sobs that were threatening to choke her, hot tears spilled down the sides of her cheeks, "when I never knew what it was like to really have a best-friend before I met you."

"You've got that giant oaf, Lina-cakes, you'll move on, I know you will. But that's the problem with me, babe, I can't. I won't ever get over losing him, I can feel it in my bones, Lina."

"You're talking like losing you will be easy for me and it won't! I don't want to lose you. I don't."

"I know this is news for you, seeing as you're one of those stubborn rich bitches, but sometimes us normal people have to do things we don't want to do." He turned his head to the side to hide his grimace. "I don't want to fight with you, babe, not right now when it's getting so cold."

"Cold," she echoed numbly. He *was* getting cold, she could feel it in the hand she held, the icy shroud of death was wrapping around him now.

"Don't bury my body, please," he begged suddenly, and maybe it was because it was close to the end, but the false confidence had left his voice, leaving him sounding young and vulnerable. "I don't want to be in the earth, I'm scared of the dark. Promise me you'll spread my ashes next to his, promise me, Lina."

"I promise," she said and that seemed to reassure him. He focused on Darius, smiling weakly.

"Bye handsome, take care of her, maybe study up on the modern world a bit."

Darius fisted his hand over his heart and spoke solemnly. "I swear."

"Jesus Christ, that's what I'm talking about right there, forget it, I'm too tired to deal with your Shakespearean arse," James said softly, and Alina squeezed his hand tighter, trying to make up for his limp grip. When they met eyes, James gave her one last crooked grin.

"Give the ring to Brigid, yeah? Should have gone to her in the first place," he muttered. With each blink of his eyes, Alina noticed it took longer and longer for him to open them again.

"James," she begged, and in that one incantation of his name she tried to pour her love, her grief, her will for him to change his mind, quickly, before it really was too late.

"S'okay, Lins, s'better this way," he slurred and then his fingers went completely slack in her grip. His eyes were open, but they weren't focused, they were turning glassy and the steady, comforting rise and fall of his chest had stilled.

"Oh god, no, no, no, no, please," Alina whimpered, a sudden rush of tears limiting her ability to speak. She pulled James's hand against her chest, cradling the limp appendage. She pressed a feather light kiss to the back of his hand, not even caring about the blood, and let the sobs wrack her body. She didn't know how long she knelt on that floor, crying over his still body, long enough to go hoarse, long enough for Darius to quit rubbing her back and start trying to pull her up to her feet.

"We must go, my Lina."

"No! I'm not leaving him! We have to carry him back with us." The sun had started to rise over the horizon, putting an end to this terrible, terrible night.

***

"Where's James?" Was the first thing Brigid asked when she met them outside and Alina couldn't seem to find the words to tell her that his body was wrapped in a spare blanket and stuffed in the back of the rental car.

Brigid seemed to take in her appearance, the dried blood crumbling off her hands, the rust colored streaks painted up almost to her elbows, the burgundy stain on her thighs, and the redness in her eyes because she asks the question again. "Where is James?"

She still couldn't find the words. Maybe her words had been all used up trying to convince James to let her save his life because she didn't have anything left in her to say to Brigid. She was hollow.

"James is dead," Darius said regretfully, "we laid his body to rest in the car."

"What." It wasn't a question.

"James is dead," Darius repeated, but it wasn't what Brigid wanted to hear.

"How? I left you three alone for twenty minutes. Twenty goddamn minutes!"

"There was a confrontation," Darius tried to explain, "James didn't make it, though he killed the man responsible for mortally wounding him."

A single strand of fiery, red hair slipped from her braid and Brigid swiped it away from her cheeks, she turned away from them, her shoulders beginning to quake. Harsh, ugly sobs filled the air between them, her chest was heaving as if they were torn physically from her body. Alina reached out towards her, to comfort, to soothe, but before she could grasp the other woman's shoulder, Brigid's hand shot out, fingers furled into a fist, and slammed them into the car's side. The skin on her knuckles split, blood trickled down her fingers and dripped into the dry earth, but Alina didn't dare try and touch her again.

"That's the third king to be lost in my lifetime," she said, and Alina could read the truth between the lines in her wavering voice. She thought it was her fault.

"Kieran's uncle, Kieran, James... none of it was your fault, Brigid," she said gently, and Brigid started shaking her head, but Alina persisted. "His uncle was old, he had no business in that fight and Kieran and James," she could feel fresh tears swell in her eyes and spill salty and hot down her cheeks, "well, they would follow each other anywhere."

Brigid cleared her throat and avoided their eyes, "we need to get his body back to the yacht, Oliver is waiting with the kids we rescued."

Darius dipped his head in agreement, "Let us leave this place before trouble follows."

***

Darius carried James's body onto his brother's boat and tucked him away inside the captain's quarters. Oliver followed him mutely and stared at the body shrouded in the sheets on his bed. He watched Alina unwrap his pale, still hand, and slid the ring from his finger.

"There's a plot on the family home I can bury him in," he finally said.

"No," she said immediately. "He's going back to Galway, he wanted to be with Kieran."

"Idiot," Oliver muttered and threw his own comforter over the body. "I could smell it on him."

"What?"

"Resignation," he explained. "As soon as he stepped on this boat, I knew he wasn't plannin' on coming back. Idiot just gave up."

"Kieran meant everything to him," she defended.

"Aye," he agreed. "He would have followed him anywhere."

Hearing such familiar words stung and the flood of sudden tears overwhelmed her. She wiped them furiously, her eyes burned, there was a sharp pain throbbing in her skull from all the crying. She felt Darius's arm wrap around her, a steady presence at her side, his voice a pleasant rumble in her ear.

"We should let him grieve, my Lina, and take the ring to Brigid," he said.

They found her up on the deck, head tilted back towards the stars, red, flaming hair down from her braids and cascading over her shoulders. She didn't acknowledge them when they approached, but the sudden stiffening in her posture meant she had heard them approach.

Alina offered her the ring, "here. He asked us to give this to you."

"Ha," she scoffed, "there's hardly any of us left. That rings brought nothing death on its kings."

"You don't want it?" Alina asked.

Brigid stared at the ring and then shook her head, "no, the kingship should die with James. We'll burn that with his body."

"I still think you should take things over, even if you don't want the ring. James thought you could rebuild and so do I," she said.

"Maybe," Brigid said vaguely and refocused her attention on the stars. "Are you coming back to the cottage?"

"No, I asked Oliver to drop Darius and I off in Dublin. I don't think I can go back there," she answered honestly.

"Not even to see him burnt?"

"I can't see that, I really can't. It was bad enough being there for Kieran's, but I can't be there for his," she said.

"Then it's doubtful we'll ever meet again," Brigid said and lowered her head to regard her seriously, "I don't regret knowing you."

Alina couldn't help but laugh, "that's high praise coming from you. I will keep in touch, I owe you, more than you know," she added.

She squeezed Brigid's elbow, knowing that was probably as much affection as the other woman would tolerate.

"And Brigid? I don't regret knowing you either."

CHAPTER 8

Alina got them a room at the first suitable looking bed and breakfast she saw. Oliver wouldn't take the other half of his payment which suited her well enough, they'd be set for weeks with that kind of cash. The sun hadn't risen when she set her bag on the bed, their little room darkened by long shadows, but Alina didn't mind, it just meant that Darius couldn't see her cry.

Maybe she thought the distance would help, but the only image her mind could seem to conjure was the silhouette of James buried under all those sheets, lying motionless on his brother's bed. His body was on its way to Galway now and here she was, sitting on a bed in Dublin. Warm hands cradled her face, wiping away the tears that fell down her cheeks.

"I shouldn't even be crying," she choked, "I'm the one that decided not to go back with him."

"You've lost a friend, we both did. It's not the kind of pain that will magically disappear, it will take years for the wound to mend, and even then, it will never really fully heal," he said.

She turned her head to the side and kissed the

soft skin of his inner wrist. She looked up at him, sniffling miserably.

"Do you think it's our fault?" she asked, "I can't stop thinking that it's our fault."

"They were in control of their own decisions, Lina, especially James, his brother-"

"I know, I remember what he said," she whispered and brought one shaking hand up to rake her fingers through the stubble on his cheek.

"Brigid will be burning him soon, distract me," she begged and parted her lips when he obliged her and slotted their mouths together.

His hands threaded through her long hair as they kissed languidly. His fingers tightened in the knot of hair at the base of her skull, sending chills sweeping down her back until her toes were curling. She decided that there were entirely too many clothes between the two of them, she missed the scorching heat of his skin and the way he ignited the fire within her.

She broke their kiss, panting in unison with the man that moved to sit across from her, and when their eyes met the air tingled with that familiar energy that their union seemed to produce. Her hands traveled down his firm chest, they found the hem of his hospital smock and tugged, indicating how badly she wanted the garment off. He obeyed immediately, tugging the ghastly white piece fabric over his head, and tossed it unceremoniously to the side.

She brought her hand back to his chest, taking

her time to explore the hard ridges of the muscles that lay beneath her fingertips. She could hear his breath catch the lower down his abdomen she trailed. Before she could continue to tease him, Darius leaned forward and captured her lips in an insistent kiss. His hands cupped her waist and he broke their kiss to lift her straight off the mattress and into his lap.

The sudden closeness and the heat emanating from his body made a pleasant, throbbing ache grow between her legs. He pressed their mouths firmly together, nipping at her plump lower lip, he used the distraction to slide his tongue between her lips, plundering her mouth until she felt the liquid heat igniting in her veins. The ache in her groin was throbbing relentlessly, she could feel herself heating up, steam rose between their parted lips.

One of his hands slid abruptly from her waist to cup one cloth covered breast. He squeezed tight and she gasped, her head unconsciously tilting back. This gave him free reign of her throat which he focused his attention on next, sucking angry red marks against her porcelain skin. His fingers around her breast loosened until they gripped her with a touch that was both firm but gentle as his tongue circled her collar bone.

Darius's thumb swept over her nipple through the thin fabric of her tunic and she jerked in his lap at the sudden, scorching touch. He swept his thumb back and forth across the sensitive nub, the material of her shirt lending just enough friction and texture to drive her crazy. She tried to squirm in his lap, desperate to relieve the tingling ache that radiated from between her legs, but his other arm was firm around her waist, locking her in place. She chewed on her abused lower lip, trying to stifle the frustrated moan that was threatening to escape, judging by the infuriating smirk on his face, he knew exactly what he was doing to her.

He released his grip on her breast to rip the shirt over the top of her head, it soon joined his in their pile on the floor. Darius's lips crashed against her own and she could feel his hand trailing down her navel, grabbing her by the waistband of her pants as he kissed her breathless.

His fingers edged between the waist of her pants, slipping down farther until his index finger was circling that little bundle of nerves that made her arch and pant into his mouth. He teased her there until she was a gasping, squirming mess before finally sinking one of his fingers into her. It wasn't quite enough to quell the throbbing ache, but she moaned anyway, hips jerking towards his finger. His finger was soon joined by another and he pumped them rhythmically, in and out, her fingers dug into the meat of his shoulders as her hips rocked in unison with his ministrations. He finally broke their kiss and her face fell against his neck, unable to hold herself up any longer while the heat grew in her belly.

Little breathy cries were drawn from between

her parted lips as Darius quickened his pace, his fingers hammering pleasure into her until all she felt was a crescendo of throbbing need that grew and grew until it exploded within her. Her orgasm tore through her, her thighs locking around his wrist, holding his fingers in place as she surrendered to a whole-body shudder. He didn't move, letting her breath as the pleasurable ache began to ebb and fade. As soon as she caught her breath, he flipped her onto her back on the mattress, ripping her pants down her milky thighs, she kicked them the rest of the way off, slipping out of her panties and kicking them aside.

Darius turned back towards her, his eyes drinking in the sight before him. He forcefully pushed his own scrub pants down his hips and crawled over her body. She could feel the firm, hot press of his arousal against her thigh. He shifted, knocking her thighs apart so he could settle in the space between them while she bent her knees to accommodate him.

One of his hands rose to gently trace the features on her face, the other planted on the mattress beside her head, keeping himself propped up. She raised her own trembling hand to brush across his cheek before bringing both hands up to cup his face. She lowered his head until she could kiss him sweetly, one hand trailing around to bury itself in the soft hair at the back of his head.

She broke the kiss and when he opened his mouth to speak, "I'm so sorry for drawing you into my life, Lina, I fear I've ruined yours."

"I'm not sorry," she said. "Even if I can never get my money back, or my home, even after all the loss...I'm not sorry because I love you enough to know I can never go back to my life before you were in it. And I don't want to hear you apologize for meeting me ever again, especially right before we have sex," she warned. "A girl could get the wrong idea," and with gentle pressure to the back of his head, she guided him into the crook of her neck. She couldn't suppress her shiver when his hot breath fanned over the sensitive skin there.

There was nothing more said between them when Darius shifted his hips forward, aligning the tip of his arousal with her slick entrance. He pressed forward, sinking every inch of himself into her tight, wet heat. He paused when he was fully seated his breath coming in heavy, quick pants against the side of her neck. She savored the sensation of feeling so full, and then tugged reassuringly on his hair, signaling him to move. With that, Darius angled his hips back away from her, slipping out almost all the way before gently pushing forward again. He set a gentle pace, the slow slide of him rubbing against her heightened nerve endings.

The pleasurable ache was building between her legs again when Darius slid his free hand between their bodies, fingers finding and squeezing her nipples. A moan left her then, her hips rolling up to meet each careful thrust. Each pinch, each squeeze, each glide of his cock sparked something deep inside her, heat began pooling behind her navel. She wrapped her legs suddenly around his hips, her ankles locking just under his backside, this sudden movement made him sink even deeper and they both gasped at the sensation. His release was sudden, and the abrupt rush of hot seed shocked her into her own orgasm. This one was slower, a wave that washed over her gradually receding to the faintest throb of pleasure.

She stroked the back of his head soothingly as they both caught their breath, and then abruptly burst into a gale of laughter. Darius lifted his head and watched her warily.

"I just thought that James would be so absolutely disgusted we did this during his funeral," she explained.

"Yes, but he wouldn't exactly be shocked."

Epilogue:

Brigid did what she set out to do, the world was

set alight with news and footage from the former Titan Corporation, and it officially became the former after the CEO and board of directors were arrested for human trafficking and child endangerment. And James was right, if anyone could reunite the last of the Fae it was Brigid, and she did. The last time Alina saw her, she was working on building homes where her people could live as a community.

That was five days ago, with her fortune back in her hands and her name cleared, she and Darius were free to go wherever they wanted. They spent the last few days at a riverside hotel in Dublin, and as shallow as it may be, Alina relished the return of luxury to her life. She spent the first day in the spa while Darius caught up on his sleep and worked her way through the entire treatment list. It was almost indescribable how it felt to get her hair and nails done after being on the run for so long.

But she didn't completely revert to the out of touch woman she had become, the first thing she did after getting access to her accounts was transfer as much money as she dared to the charities responsible for cleaning up the mess Titan had left behind. She made sure to funnel funds to Brigid, even beyond what she owed her people, though the fiery woman had expressly told her that her people didn't need handouts. Admittedly, Alina may have gone overboard, but that was how she had learned to solve problems, just throw money at them.

It took a few days, but she also brought flowers to the stone marker where Brigid had scattered James's ashes next to Kieran's. She didn't cry this time, but she still felt the loss all the same. Felt it in the silence that seemed to haunt her, felt it in the sheer wrongness that wrapped around her like a shroud whenever she waited for James to comment on something particularly funny or strange that she saw, but the comments never came. In the short time that they had known each other, he filled a void in her that she didn't even know she had.

The sliding glass door opened with a quiet 'whoosh' as Darius stepped out to join her on the balcony. Strong arms encircled her waist, his head tilted and resting lightly a top hers as he joined her watching the sun set. Arrows of orange and golden light streaked the river, a mirror image of the splotchy painter's sky above, and Alina felt warmth blossom over her body, chasing away the hollow cold.

"Where do you want to go next?" Darius asked softly.

"Romania," she answered at once. "I still have some questions about myself that need answered. Are you up for one more adventure?"

She felt his head move against hers as he turned and kissed the side of her head, "you should know by now I would follow you anywhere. Let's see where this adventure takes us, shall we?"

End

BONUS SHORT: JAMES AND KIERAN'S STORY

"Would you like to come for a drink with me?" Kieran regretted the offer almost as soon the words left his lips.

The already inebriated man in front of him squinted his rather lovely blue-gray eyes and seemed to regard Kieran for a moment, giving him an obvious once over. He must have liked what he saw because in the next instant he was straightening back up and trying to wipe some of the drying blood off his face.

"You askin' me out on a date?" He leered, his accent thicker after the beating he'd just received.

"Whiskey'll help with the pain," Kieran said instead of answering.

"You're askin' me on a date, aren't you?" He asked once more, this time with a wry grin. He squinted at him again, "you paying?"

"Of course, I was the one who invited you, wasn't I?" Kieran said.

"All right then," the blond agreed easily and slung an arm around Kieran's shoulders. "Where are we off too?"

"There's a pub round the corner," Kieran said and began to walk with the unruly, taller man. He kept trying to scrub the drying blood from his nose and chin with the back of his free hand, keeping an endless stream of chatter all the while.

"What's your name?" Kieran interrupted softly and was met with an easy smile that did funny things to his stomach.

"James, what's yours then? I guess it's pretty shite of me not to ask the name of my dashing hero, 'specially' after he's going to be payin' for my drinks like a real gentleman," he said.

"My name is Kieran, but I'm not really a hero. I'm sure you could have handled yourself on your own," he finished awkwardly.

"Are you kidding? I was getting my arse kicked, mate," he said, and he wasn't really wrong, Kieran was just trying to be polite. He remembered very clearly what it had looked like when he stumbled across the blond getting beaten down in the alley way, but he would never forget the way his eyes-

shone steely blue-grey with so much fight that Kieran knew he'd be beaten to death before the thought of backing down and running ever crossed his mind. The three men in the alley were pummeling him, fists cracking against his jaw, his nose, another kicking him over and over in the ribs as he stared up at them defiantly.

The oldest, looking like he was in his mid-to-late thirties with his scraggly brown beard and beer gut that jiggled with every hit to the blond, cracked his fist once more across the handsome mans face and then reared back to spit on his huddled, prone form.

"Ready to take back what you said about my baby brother, fag?" He snarled.

But the blond only broke out in painful laughter, "even if I took it back, it wouldn't change the fact that your brother's been fuckin' me for weeks," he cackled.

That earned him another 'crack'! across the face from Mr. Beer Gut.

"You take it back! Take it back you nasty little cocksucking fairy!" He screamed uncomfortably close to the blond's face.

"Hey," Kieran said as he crossed the threshold into the mouth of the alley, "what's going on here, fellas?"

"Oh, stay out of it, you stupid mick," the man said and reared his fist back to hit the blond again, only this time Kieran was there to catch him by the wrist.

He tsked softly, "now that wasn't very polite, now was it?"

The larger man tried to jerk his arm out of Kieran's vice-like grip, but he held firm. Maybe it wasn't a fair fight with Kieran's fae blood burning hot, giving him supernatural strength, but neither was three-against-one. He tightened his fingers around the man's meaty wrist and tried to stamp down the sick pleasure that rose in his gut watching him squirm. The other two men were clearly intimidated that he could keep their leader down because they had skittered a few steps away from the blond man, eyeing the mouth of the alley uncertainly. Kieran gave the fat man's arm a shake.

"I think you better apologize to the young man, then you best be on your way home," Kieran said.

"Fuck you," the man spat, and Kieran clamped down on his wrist until he could feel the bones grinding together.

"Okay, okay!" He screamed and grit his teeth together, "sorry...musta' been a misunderstanding."

"The fuck it was," the blond man said and rolled quickly back to his feet. Before Kieran realized what was happening, he had grabbed the lid from a nearby upturned garbage bin and cracked the fatter man over the head with it. He dropped face first into the slimy pavement and then the blond man was grabbing Kieran by the wrist, hauling him away as he cackled.

"Quick! Before that fat fucker manages to lumber up to his feet," he cried and dragged him back out to the road where there were still people on their way to dinner or getting off work. He stopped, bent double at the waist as he heaved in air, hands balanced on his knees, blond hair flopping over his eyes, and blood dripping from his nose. He looked up at Kieran and beamed and that split second was all it took for Kieran to realize he was staring at the most beautiful man he had ever met.

"Hey," the blond began,-

"you okay, mate?"

"Sorry, what?" Kieran asked.

"You kinda spaced out for a minute there, mate.

Stopped walking and everything," James said.

"Sorry, it's right around the corner here. What're you drinking?"

"Jameson, straight obviously," James eyed him suspiciously, "you're going to order some sort of embarrassingly fruity cocktail, aren't you?"

"Well, I-maybe I just like the little umbrella."

James cackled, "s'okay, I'm cool enough for the two of us."

***

What a disaster that turned out to be. The already inebriated man only became even drunker, taking at least four shots while Kieran's back was turned, and hitting on the barman incessantly until they were eventually thrown out. By that time Kieran was sure James had consumed more than just four shots by the way the other man was hanging off him, in spite of being about a head taller.

Despite James plastered against his side, arms thrown over his shoulders as Kieran literally drug him towards the inn he was staying, complaining drunkenly in his ear that the barman hadn't returned his attentions, Kieran still didn't regret asking him. He didn't mind James's beautiful accented voice as it lilted through his complaints, or the smell of his cologne mixing enticingly with his natural scent until every breath Kieran took reminded him of being at the ocean. He really didn't mind the press of the blond's long, slender body against his side.

He finally got them up to the door of his room, trying to juggle James and the key when he felt long, creeping fingers fiddle with the front of his fly. He was barely able to fumble and grab the other man's wrist right as he felt those long fingers wriggle their way into the front of his trousers. He curled his hand firmly around his slender wrist, feeling the delicate bones under the skin.

"What are you doing?!" He cried, just managing to get the door open.

"Gonna give you a handie," James mumbled, his face squashed against Kieran's neck.

"You're drunk," Kieran said firmly and eased his hand out of his trousers, shoving him through the door.

This had the disastrous effect of sending him sprawled across the threshold of Kieran's room. When he reached to help him up, James was already on his knees, grabbing Kieran's thighs to steady himself, leaving him eye level with Kieran's crotch. James tilted his head up at him, lavascious smirk painted on his mouth.

"If you wanted a blowie instead you should have just asked," he purred and swayed forward, nuzzling into the front of his trousers.

Kieran felt his body begin to respond to the stimuli, his cock swelling at the sight of James on his knees in front of him, lips moist, eyes gleaming mischievously. It took all the willpower he possessed to back away and put some distance between them.

"You're drunk," he reiterated.

"So?" James whined, slumping miserably back on his heels, "what does that matter? I'm drunk an' horny and you've been a proper gentleman tonight."

"You're drunk and I'm not," Kieran continued before James could interrupt, "it would be taking advantage of you and that's not how I want our relationship to start."

"Relationship?" James blurted in a small voice.

Kieran rubbed the back of his neck, cheeks flushing, "this isn't really how I imagined asking you out again, but yeah, I want to keep seeing you, if you'll have me."

"No ones ever asked me on a second date before," James admitted, "and I know I'm a bit of a slut, y'know? I always put out, so you don't have to try so hard, mate, I'm right here."

"I don't want to just have sex with you," he said, "I want to know you."

"Why?" James asked softly.

"You're the most interesting person I've ever met," he said honestly.

"Will you ask me again?"

"What?" Kieran asked.

"On that second date, will you ask me again? So, I know I haven't dreamt it," he explained.

"In the morning," Kieran agreed, "now let's get you into bed."

"Will you stay with me?"

"You don't even have to ask, 'course I will, darlin'" he said and pretended he didn't see James brighten at the use of the pet name.

Later, when they were both laying facing one another and Kieran was watching his chest rise and fall in peaceful slumber, he idly twirled a strand of blond hair between his fingers and marveled how soft it was. He wondered how many men had used James and then discarded him for the other man to say things like that about himself. It only made Kieran want to prove him wrong, and he'd start with breakfast at the café the sleeping man had mumbled about as he was drifting off. Kieran had been there before and found their breakfast menu a little too on the sweet side for his liking, but he already had the feeling he'd follow James anywhere.

End

Dear Reader,

Firstly, thank you for taking this journey with me. Secondly, if you enjoyed this series, don't forget to rate and review! And Thirdly, I'm debating a prequel standalone featuring a more in depth look at Kieran and James and their journey together, let me know in your review if you think I should go for it.

I'll see in our next adventure,

Evie

ABOUT THE AUTHOR

Evelyn Winters

Evelyn Winters lives in rural Idaho with her two cats. She grew up reading Fantasy and Science Fiction, and loves writing romance with a paranormal or fantastical twist. When she isn't writing, she can be found drinking too much coffee and binge reading romance novels.

If you want to connect you can reach Evelyn at evelynwinterswrites@gmail.com or https://twitter.com/EveWintersBooks

BOOKS BY THIS AUTHOR

Guardian Of Bear Creek

Amelia is a woman tormented by her past and an ex-husband who just won't let go. She risks everything when she flees to a rural town in Eastern Oregon, but the place she calls her salvation is harboring a secret of its own. She thought she was done with men, too broken, too jaded, but Eli makes her want to pick up the pieces of her shattered life and move on.

Eli has a job to do, one that's passed down from father to son for generations. He's not looking for distractions when he meets Amelia at the local diner, but his bear is drawn to her, and he can't help but be captivated by the strength that seems to be holding the fragile woman together.

When Amelia's past hunts her down, Eli's protective fury and her own hidden strength isn't enough to save the new lovers. Will the secret hidden in the mountains be enough to save them?

Guardian Of Lone Wolf Peak

Kira always knew who she was: the broken stepdaughter of a failed construction contractor with a mean streak, but things were changing and she might not be as broken as she thought she was. When things between her and her step-father finally come to a head, Kira's life is turned upside down and she's forced to run away from the life she had before.

Sent to live in her best friend's family cabin, Kira tries to unravel one mystery after another. But the most shocking revelation? The four brothers she's been sent to live with might not be entirely human.

There's Charles, the leader. He's stubborn, powerful, and deeply loyal to his family, but he's keeping his own secret locked up inside the family's property.

Nathan is the secretive second in command. He's tall and handsome, and as agile as a timber wolf, but he doesn't warm up to strangers easily.

Benji is the youngest, he has a smile that radiates warmth like the sun and is equally as hot-tempered. What's more is he seems determined that

Kira belongs with him though she tries to hold him at arms length.

Then there's Nick, the rebellious outcast made from shadows and sin. Half the time Kira could believe that he hates her and she would say the same if it didn't feel like every cell in her body was trying to draw him in.

Can Kira untangle the web of secrets that shroud this picturesque cabin in the woods? Or will she even want to know when the answer may crush her budding romance with one of the brothers?

Escape From Lone Wolf Peak

Kira's story continues in the sequel to Guardian of Lone Wolf Peak.

On the run from the police after a brutal encounter with her cruel step-father, Kira escaped to the mountains and the secret family home owned by her best friend Chloe and occupied by Chloe's four sinfully attractive brothers. She felt an instant connection with Nick, a passion that threatened to burn them both if they gave into their desires.

But what her friend didn't tell her was the dark secret her family was harboring. Her loyalties are tested when she's warned of the cruel fate Nick's brother's have in store for her by a mysterious stranger who's been visiting her dreams.

Will Kira escape Lone Wolf Peak or will she succumb to the alpha's demands?

The Guardians Of Eternal: Books 1-3 With Bonus Short

The first three novellas in the Guardians of Eternal series plus bonus short: Ezra's Story.

Novellas include:

Guardian of Bear Creek

Guardian of Lone Wolf Peak

Escape From Lone Wolf Peak

Plus Bonus Short!

Manufactured by Amazon.ca
Bolton, ON